Mad About the Man

Also by Stella Cameron
in Large Print:

Pure Delights
Guilty Pleasures
More and More
Finding Ian

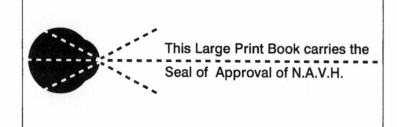

This Large Print Book carries the
Seal of Approval of N.A.V.H.

Mad About the Man

Stella Cameron

WHEELER
PUBLISHING

Published in 2003 by arrangement with Harlequin Books, S.A.

Wheeler Large Print Compass Series.

The text of this Large Print edition is unabridged.
Other aspects of the book may vary from the original edition.

Set in 16 pt. Plantin by Liana M. Walker.

Printed in the United States on permanent paper.

ISBN 1-58724-402-0 (lg. print : hc : alk. paper)

For Ann Maxwell, a woman of vision

Prologue

"Taste it, Jacques, *taste* it."

"Convince me I want to."

Rita laughed and leaned closer. "Let your tongue convince you, darling. We both know what a voluptuary you are."

"Mmm. Voluptuaries enjoy being persuaded." He watched her fingers move — slender, clever fingers practiced in the small nuances of temptation. "Show me how good you are. Make me want what you're offering so badly it hurts."

Her subtle scent reached him — summer roses. Jacques let his eyelids drift down a fraction. Creamy roses. Curving petals that begged to be cupped, just as the velvet fullness of a passionate woman's breasts begged to be cupped by a lover's hands.

Soft breath touched his face. She was very near. "I can make you want this, Jacques. Open your mouth."

"You haven't convinced me."

"But I *have* aroused your jaded appetites, haven't I? Go with me, Jacques. Let me lead you. Let me *seduce* you."

"I've always made a better leader than a follower."

Her smile was lazy. "I've never met a sensual man who couldn't be turned on by a little female mastery. Forced seduction, Jacques. Come on, don't tell me it'll be the first time you were taken rather than the taker."

"You could be right. Why don't you tell me exactly how you intend to do it, sweetheart? Guide me through, step by step."

"My pleasure." Moistening her lips with the pointed tip of her pink tongue, Rita rested a forearm on his thighs. "First we do a little touching."

"Do we?"

"Oh, yes. Textures excite, Jacques. You know that. Sensation is everything."

Oh, yeah. "I'm bored, Rita. Can you give me sensations that'll help me forget just how bored I am?"

"Guaranteed. Relax." Her fingertips stroked little circles. "I guess I missed a step. Before we can touch we have to get rid of the wrappings. To touch, we need *naked*, Jacques, naked things the tongue wants to curl around."

"Naked is one of my favorite words."

Now Rita held her tongue between her teeth and went to her knees between his legs. "I'm going to loosen this, Jacques — it'll help you get deeper into the mood. Aah . . ."

8

She tossed back her hair and those nimble fingers went to work again. "Better? Do I have your attention now?"

"I'm only human," he murmured and shifted in his seat. "How long is this going to take?"

"In a hurry now?"

"Let's just say I feel something's going to present itself at any second and I'm not going to be able to avoid dealing with it."

"Ah, Jacques — you do live up to your reputation. Always ready to go. I'm ready, too, darling. Open your mouth."

"Why?"

"Because I've got something you're going to want to fill it with." She peeled away satiny red and silken white. "See. Can you tell me these aren't perfect enough to make a man hungry?"

"Rita —"

"Open your mouth."

Sighing, he did as she asked.

"Come on. Draw it in. *Yes. Yes!* Oh, *yes!* That's the way."

Jacques closed his eyes.

"Ah, ah, ah. Slowly, darling, slowly. Make it last. Roll your tongue around it and over it and . . . *Yes!* Tell me you like it, Jacques. Tell me you can't get enough of it. Sweetheart, there's plenty more where that came from."

He swallowed and looked into her flushed face. "Nice try, Rita. You gave it your best shot. If anyone could breathe some life into me, it's you."

"But?" With a thump, she sat on her heels. "*But,* Jacques? Don't do this to me. I can't stand it."

"You're going to have to. I just can't get it up anymore — the enthusiasm is gone. It's been gone for a long time. I'm bored with the whole process."

"You can't be." She pouted.

"Oh, but I can. Watch my lips while I make the words, sweetheart."

Frowning, Rita crossed her arms. "I'm watching."

"If I ever have to taste another candy I'm going to puke."

1

"No! He's not getting away with it!"

"Gaby, Gaby, don't *do* this to yourself." Char Brown, elderly, graying and oozing creative talent, trotted in Gaby McGregor's wake.

"Take *one* man, add *too* much money and not enough to do with it — or with his time — and what d'you have?"

"Gaby —"

"I'll tell you what you have. *Trouble.* Trouble with a capital *T.*"

Char edged rapidly around Gaby and faced her in the window of the millinery workroom. "Forget Jacques Ledan. Forget the whole issue. You can't stop a man like him."

"He wants to turn Goldstrike into some sort of destination tourist trap." Frustration boiled in Gaby. "Char, he's *buying* this town. He plans to form one great big club and we're all getting a membership whether we like it or not. It's going to be 'join or leave.' I'm not leaving, and I'm not giving up on this without a fight."

"Let it go. Who buys what in this town

11

and what they do with it isn't your problem."

"It *is* my problem. It's a problem for every one of us who lives here. Things may be financially depressed, but we're used to that. Great as Knott's Berry Farm is, we don't want to become California's next down-home fun spot."

"Gaby, this isn't something you can change."

"The hell it isn't! I live here. My best friends live here. Hell, my *daughter* lives here!" And for the first time in her life, Gaby really liked where she was and who she was with.

"Gaby, what's happened to your language?"

"Once the rot gets in it spreads. First he bought up the old schoolhouse. Then Bartlett's Feed Store. . . . I'm not the only one who thinks they'd have held on if he hadn't made an offer they couldn't refuse. Next it'll be the abandoned fire station. He'll gobble up any little businesses that go under —" she paused for breath "— and on and on until Goldstrike looks like Carmel, only tackier."

"You're getting carried away." Char's dark eyes were bright with worry. "He'll never make it work, anyway. And a lot of people think Carmel's cute. It's got Clint Eastwood. But this *isn't* Carmel. We don't *have* an ocean to run to. This is central California

12

and it's dirt, yellow, plain — and everyone knows it."

"The *hell* — I happen to like the way this little town looks." In fact, she loved it, had adored it from that first day, almost six years ago, when she'd been on a trip going nowhere, coming from nowhere she wanted to go back to, and had stopped for gas. The radiator in her old Chevy station wagon had chosen that moment to spring a leak, and a gas stop turned into an overnight stay that led to a permanent address change — for Gaby and her then year-old daughter, Mae.

And Gaby *loved* the place.

"I like Goldstrike, too," Char said quietly. She jabbed a pin repeatedly into the cushion she wore on a band around her wrist — a sure sign she was more upset than she wanted Gaby to guess. "Forget Jacques Ledan and his megaresort plans. Think fruit. Keep your mind on fruit. This is the year of the fruit theme at Gaby's. Fruit is great." She snatched up a black velvet pillbox-shaped hat and coiled a spray of silk strawberries on the crown.

For a moment the only sound in the room was the whir of wooden blades in the overhead fans.

"The fruit is great?" Gaby said carefully, narrowing eyes she'd been told, usually by people not destined to be great friends, could resemble green drill bits.

13

"Great," Char repeated. "Absolutely." She nodded the mass of wiry, gray-peppered dark curls that reached her shoulders.

Gaby settled a hat on her head and pulled the straight brim far down over her eyes. The black straw matador number had a band fashioned from a string of miniature wax bananas. "Yesterday," she said deliberately, "yesterday the fruit stank. Today it's great. Did you get a brain transplant since you stepped out of here last night, or what?"

Char hunched her thin shoulders. "I thought it through, okay?"

"Not okay." Giving the hat brim an added downward tilt, Gaby dropped into a chair. She had made wearing her own creations a trademark. Every day a different hat. She pointed at Char. "I know diversion tactics when I see them. They won't work. Ooh, wait till I get my hands on this bozo."

"He owns Ledan Confectionery and he's no bozo. You can't call a multimillionaire a bozo."

Gaby raised her jaw. She knew the hat suited her. With her long, straight black hair drawn back from a finely boned face dominated by great green eyes and a full mouth, her inner eye told her exactly the picture she made: dramatically elegant. She wasn't vain, just savvy. If customers liked what they saw on her, they wanted to duplicate the effect for themselves. That sold

14

hats and that was her business. Goldstrike was a small town, once a gold-panning settlement, that had been dying for longer than any of the current inhabitants remembered. Fruit farmers and the handful of businesses needed to support them; that's what Goldstrike was about. These people didn't need fancy hats. But there were women among them who needed and wanted the work Gaby's one-woman whirlwind operation could provide, and the whole town benefited from the people who traveled long distances just to buy and own a genuine "Gaby." Those customers came, spent enough money to be of slight help to Goldstrike's economy and left. And they didn't stay long enough to change anything the natives didn't want disturbed.

"I think," Gaby said after consideration, "that there's absolutely no reason I can't call some idiot from Los Angeles a bozo just because he's got a gold-plated rear."

Char tossed aside the black velvet and grabbed her iced tea. "You're going downhill, my girl. You're losing it. Gold-plated rear?"

"Yeah. He wallowed in money so long it worked its way through his skin, and since he made his bucks in candy, he's gotta be a taddy bit porky, which means he has to sit on his rear a lot because he's too tired to move. Gravity pulls, right?"

"Uh-huh." Char crossed her arms.

"Right. Okay. So a lot of the money in his skin turned to gold and sank to the lowest point of gravity. His backside is pure fourteen carat and since money is what occupies his brain — one hundred percent — that's where his brain is. What would *you* call a guy who keeps his brain there?"

"All the years you lived with that wild crowd in Los Angeles spoiled you."

"Probably." They certainly caused her to marry a man because he looked good enough to eat, even though he had nothing in common with her. But without Michael there wouldn't have been a Mae, so she guessed she wouldn't change a thing about all of that. "Don't forget it's the Los Angeles contacts who keep us going up here. And you and I found each other in LA. Have you met this Ledan guy?"

"No."

"Who has?"

Char frowned and shook her head.

"Someone must have. He's been all over town trying to buy up real estate."

"No one's mentioned actually meeting him."

Gaby sniggered. "Like I told you. He sits in his Los Angeles office . . . or his Paris office or up there in that great big ugly house of his in *our* mountains —" she indicated the nearby foothills of the Sierra Nevada "— and that's all he does . . . sit. And think up ways to make even more money and make our lives miserable in the process. He can't even get out and do his own dirty work."

"I'm sure the man doesn't deliberately try to dream up things we won't like."

"No. He doesn't think about us at all. We don't exist to Mr. Jacques Ledan. Ooh, I hate him. I may just go up and speak to him myself. Once he sees what he's up against he may decide to take his resort and . . . take it elsewhere."

Char laughed. "You are pretty terrifying."

"I may not look particularly . . . robust, but I can stand up for myself." Gaby glowered at the other woman. All her life she'd been told how fragile she looked, and she detested being seen as a delicate, exotic flower of a woman. Her personality was anything but soft.

A distant jingle sounded. The workroom was behind a small showroom that fronted on the street. Locals came to the back entrance. The bell announced a customer.

Char looked surprised. "Another drop-in? Two in one day?" Since Goldstrike wasn't on a main highway, very few sales were to casual customers.

"Your turn," Gaby said quickly.

"Uh-uh." Char picked up the strawberry vine once more. "I took the other one. This is your chance to shine." She flipped the brilliantly striped skirt of her loose cotton dress and sat down, tucking thin, brown ankles around the legs of her chair.

Without another word, Gaby got up and swept between empty worktables. On Saturdays she and Char worked alone and traded off turns dealing with any buyers.

Entering the shop, her flat sandals making slapping sounds on stone tiles, Gaby was confronted by a tall, auburn-haired woman with penetrating brown eyes, a full figure in a red suit, noticeably good legs all the way down to high, high-heeled red shoes . . . and a frown that would compete with Gaby's renowned best efforts. To the woman's left, apparently fascinated by one of the hats in the window, stood a huskily built blond man. A flash of sun on a tinted windshield drew attention to a navy-blue limousine outside.

"Good morning." Gaby looked from the pointed-crowned, claret-colored velvet evening hat the woman balanced on a forefinger, to those piercing eyes. "Looking for something for the theater . . . the opera, perhaps?"

The claret hat featured a swathe of net veiling dotted with tiny crystal beads and discreetly edged with shiny red currants. Gaby was very pleased with her fruit theme.

"Who on earth wears something like this around here?" The woman's voice held no malice, only genuine curiosity.

Gaby hitched at the slipping shoulders of her wide-necked overblouse. "No one around here does." She didn't bother to add that the congresswoman who'd ordered the hat would wear it at a gala charity concert in Washington.

"Oh." The woman's gaze slid from Gaby to the hat and back to Gaby. "I see. Are you Gaby McGregor?"

"The same."

The man, thirtyish, blue-eyed and boyishly handsome, aimed a charming smile in Gaby's direction before settling into a black wicker chair meant more for decoration than actual use.

"You don't look . . . Are you from Goldstrike?" the woman asked.

"Oh, yes. This is home." She didn't owe anyone her life history, particularly not some overdressed fruitcake.

"I'm Rita Nagel." Still balancing the conical hat on her left forefinger, the way a plate juggler would, the woman thrust out her right hand.

Gaby shook hands, not without noting long, perfectly manicured nails . . . and a surprisingly firm grip. "Hi, Rita."

"How many people work for you?"

The question took Gaby aback. "Um — it varies, depending upon the orders." She wasn't about to tell her the exact number.

19

Rita Nagel eyed the flashy creation on her finger. "I guess your people fiddle around with stuff like this when there isn't enough to do."

Her own frown, Gaby was certain, must rival Rita's. "Not exactly." Almost every hat in the showroom had been commissioned. They were merely kept there for convenience and to act as window dressing when people came to pick up orders.

Sighing, Rita set the hat down on one of the gold wire, head-shaped cages that were arranged in spotlighted alcoves around the shop.

"I think you're going to be very interested in my reason for being here," Rita said, a tight smile jerking up the corners of her small, red mouth. "I expect you'd love to be busy enough to need every one of your employees full-time — and then some."

The man beat a tattoo on the tiles with the toes of his shiny, Gucci loafers. Dressed in a fashionably relaxed-looking gray linen suit, a khaki shirt and beige tie, he would definitely be much more at home on Rodeo Drive.

"Ms. McGregor?"

Gaby dragged her attention from the silent, smiling man. "Yes?" Someone should tell Rita about making introductions — if he couldn't make them himself.

"You've probably heard the name Jacques

Ledan." Rita inclined her head toward her companion.

Gaby stared at Ledan with unwilling curiosity. "Probably," she told Rita without enthusiasm.

"Are you aware of his proposed project in Goldstrike?"

"Project?" She darted a glance at the blond man, who nodded pleasantly.

"So you don't know very much." Rita's eyes took on the glaze of a woman experiencing a satisfying inner vision. "Mr. Ledan is a very forward-thinking man. I'm sure you've heard of Ledan Confectionery."

How forward thinking did you have to be to keep on making the candy your family had been selling forever? "I've heard of it."

"What's your favorite?" Ledan's mellow, all-American accent surprised Gaby. He turned his blue eyes toward the ceiling. "Let me guess. You're either a Latin Lover's Cordial or — and this is probably the one — Sinful Sensations." His smile shone upon her once more. "For the woman who likes a selection?"

Gaby detested glib men . . . particularly glib, *egocentric* men. "I guess you haven't noticed that in Goldstrike we're strictly on the simple side. Around here it's a treat to buy caramel apples at Artie's Grocery. This is definitely not the place to come if you're a Ledan's type."

"It will be," the man said, grinning complacently.

She hated him . . . had already hated him. Now she detested the man.

Rita snapped her fingers for attention. "As I was saying, Mr. Ledan is a man of vision. He sees potential in this town. And need. He intends to make it his mission to bring Goldstrike into the twentieth century."

Almost too amazed to respond, Gaby eyed Rita's fingers, still poised in snapping mode. "I'm very busy . . . so if you don't mind . . ."

"Using all you little local people." Rita continued without missing a beat. "That's part of Mr. Ledan's plan. I'm his assistant and he wants me to approach those tradespeople in the town whom we've already identified as having some useful contribution to make — for Mr. Ledan and for their own benefit."

Gaby avoided looking at Ledan. "Is there any reason why he can't be the one to tell us little people what he has in mind?"

"He is. Through me."

"Has he suddenly lost the gift of speech?"

"Mr. Ledan doesn't deal with these things directly. He hires people to carry out his wishes — like me."

Rather than show the pair of them the door, Gaby decided the wiser course would be to gather as much information as possible about Ledan's "project" plans.

Rita was smiling, showing small, perfect

teeth. "Eventually Mr. Ledan hopes to find things for all the existing local businesses to do. He wants every one of you to feel truly cared about and involved in what he intends to do for you."

Gaby couldn't form a single complete sentence of response.

"I can see you're overwhelmed. I can well understand that you must be." Rita hitched a shapely hip onto the desk where Gaby did all her paperwork and crossed one long, elegant leg over the other. She pulled a notebook from her red Chanel purse and flipped it open. "Gaby's. You make hats."

Make hats! Not, you are a millinery designer! Not, you are currently negotiating a contract to design hats for the upcoming movie musical *Going to the Dogs.*

"Ms. McGregor?"

Gaby swung wide her arms to encompass the showroom filled with hats. "I suppose you might say I make hats, yes."

"Well —" Rita's white teeth flashed "— this is your lucky day. Mr. Ledan is looking for simple items that can be produced in small quantities at first, then mass-produced later. Of course, for the mass production we'll have to go to a professional."

Gaby choked back an exclamation.

"You're astounded," Rita said. "Understandable, but you'll discover that Mr. Ledan is very generous. Too generous sometimes. People try to take advantage of him. But he'd like to commission you to make baseball caps."

"Baseball caps?" Heat climbed steadily up Gaby's neck.

"Yes, you know the sort of thing. Like the baseball players wear."

"Baseball players?"

"Exactly. We'll need them in small, medium and large and we've decided on green."

"Green." This had to be a bad dream — or a bad joke.

"Mmm. With the logo GFTG above the word Goldstrike. I expect you've already guessed what GFTG stands for." Rita giggled — an unlikely sound.

"Surprise me," Gaby said through stiff lips.

"Go for the Gold!" Rita wiggled delightedly. "Go for the Gold in Goldstrike. With a little rainbow popping into a pot of gold. Isn't that clever? At first we intend to send the caps out to publicity people and so on. In time everyone who *is* anyone will have come to Goldstrike to find their little bit of gold and they'll all be wearing GFTG hats. And *you* will always know that the very first ones were made right here in your little factory."

Factory! Gaby breathed slowly and carefully through her nose. She spared a glance for Ledan only to find him deeply engrossed in Rita's spectacular legs. "Why would GFTG ever come to mean anything but winning

24

Olympic medals — to anyone but Mr. Ledan? And you, of course."

Rita tutted and shook her head pityingly. "I mustn't forget what a quiet life you lead in a place like this. I suppose it might be nice to be cut off from it all — for about a day. TV, of course! We'll be doing commercial spots eventually. And radio and print. The whole country will know what's happening here. The rainbow with the pot of gold is perfect. Guides — you know, the people who will show visitors around — they'll be dressed as leprechauns, and we're going to have a series of fixed mining displays showing carefully accurate mining procedures." Rita leaned closer and her wavy auburn hair swung forward. "The equipment will be accurate, but we're going to dress the models of miners like leprechauns, too! Leprechauns with miners' lamps on their heads!"

A picture, a ghastly nightmarish picture of oversized leprechauns leaping down Goldstrike's two business streets and between the scattering of public buildings, houses and trailer parks that composed the entire settlement, stunned Gaby.

Ledan finally broke his silence. "You're really bowled over, aren't you? We've got a long, long way to go before we can declare this thing a success, but with responses like yours I'm convinced this is going to be really something."

Remain calm, Gaby ordered herself. She closed her eyes for a moment and deliberately ironed all expression from her face.

"Are you all right?" Ledan asked, sounding concerned.

"Yes, I am." She raised her chin. "I certainly am." Combatting the kind of power this man represented would take organization and a lot of levelheaded thinking. Blowing her top in front of him would accomplish nothing. "Thank you for stopping by."

"But —"

Gaby raised a silencing hand to Rita. "No, no. Don't say another word. I'm going back into the workroom now. Quietly. Then I'm going to go through everything you've said to me." *To make certain she didn't forget a word the rest of the locals would want to hear.*

"But —"

"Please!" Gaby walked between Rita and Ledan. "I definitely need to be alone. Absolutely alone for a while. I'm sure you can find your way out."

As she passed into the short hallway leading to the workroom she heard Rita say, "Odd person. I guess living in a burg like this might make your tolerance for excitement real low. Do you think she's angry?"

"Come on, Rita," Ledan said. "Let's get back. Like I already said, she's bowled over. Imagine being in her shoes. Imagine living here all your life. Then think how you'd react to hearing you were about to become part of the biggest thing that ever happened in your little world."

"I don't know. She looked angry to me."

Rita wasn't a complete dummy after all.

"Not at all. Just try to visualize —"

Gaby shut the door to the workroom firmly behind her and leaned against it. Ledan, on the other hand, might well be a dummy — a dummy with money — a terrible prospect. "Char." She covered her face with her hands, then dropped them to her sides. "Char, you are never going to believe this. That creep . . . Char?"

The workroom was empty. A piece of paper flapped from the cork head form they used as a bulletin board. Muttering, Gaby went to rip it off. Char's elegant handwriting announced that she had gone over to Sis's, the town's diner and primary meeting spot, the only place in Goldstrike that served food — unless you counted Barney's burners, the tacos sold at the local tavern.

Gaby thought of Sis, sixty and full of energy, sister of three burly, silent older brothers who were fruit farmers. Sis's was the center of everything in Goldstrike and had been, so Gaby was told, since Sis's brothers bought her the diner to take her mind off the trucker who passed through and broke her heart — forty years earlier. What place could

Sis possibly have in Ledan's damnable Leprechaun City?

And Barney who ran the Hacienda Heaven — known as Barney's Bar until he returned from a trip to Tijuana twenty years ago. Barney served tacos made of whatever he could buy cheaply and douse liberally in hot sauce. What would Ledan's plans be for him?

If this curse of a "project" ever got off the ground, it would change the face of Goldstrike forever.

"I won't let it," Gaby said, pressing the thumbtack back into the cork head until a screwdriver would be needed to extract it again. "No way."

She sat at a worktable, turned over Char's note and began jotting. "GFTG in Goldstrike." It was *horrible!*

The jangle of the shop bell, distant through the door she'd closed, made her hands curl into fists. She got up very slowly and walked toward the showroom. If they'd come back she'd need every fragment of her control not to let them know what she thought of their "project."

She opened the door and felt instantly relieved. The man standing in almost the same spot where Ledan had stood had dark hair.

Gaby paused on the threshold to the shop. This man was tall, very tall . . . and broadshouldered . . . and slimhipped . . . and

28

dressed completely in black.

He was intent on something outside the window. Gaby looked beyond him, but saw only the quiet street and the hair salon opposite, its stucco walls turned gold by a low, October-afternoon sun. A Jeep, in shades of army olive drab, was parked at the curb.

There was something about his stance: alert, poised as if ready to pounce . . . or strike. Gaby's stomach went into a dive. Her heartbeat thudded in her ears.

Rita Nagel had said she thought Gaby was angry. Perhaps she'd persuaded Ledan she was right, and now they'd sent someone to make sure Gaby would be more enthusiastic about Leprechaunville in the future.

He turned his head slightly, showing a high cheekbone and hard jaw. The tip of his eyebrow flared upward and a faint nimbus formed about slightly lowered lashes. His thick curly hair reached his collar and was as black as Gaby's; maybe blacker. A black shirt hugged a muscular back and biceps and fitted, hand-tailored close, all the way to the black belt at the waist of snug black pants.

The stomach dive became a loop. Nothing about him moved.

A shiver ran up Gaby's spine. She crossed her arms tightly. Once before, she'd felt an instant aura of raw power emanating from a man, but on that occasion it hadn't happened until she'd seen his face.

She took another step into the shop. At the same moment a truck rumbled by, and the man watched its progress, turning until she saw his full profile. His nose was straight, his bottom lip fuller than the upper. Even in repose, the corner of his mouth tilted up and a vertical groove showed in his cheek. The sleeves of his shirt were rolled back over tanned, muscular forearms, and a slim gold watch glistened at his wrist where he rested his hands on his hips.

Gaby slowly shifted a hand to her stomach and pressed. Once before. Never again. And she was being foolish. This was a total stranger who probably wanted nothing more complicated than to ask directions.

So why wouldn't he choose the gas station over a millinery shop?

He flexed his spine and looked over his shoulder . . . directly at Gaby.

Her hands slid slowly to her sides. His eyes, in a deeply tanned face, were dark, dark blue. Full-face, the uptilted mouth — so very seriously set — was wide and firm. The vertical lines rose to his cheekbones, and there was a definite cleft in the center of his square chin. A black tie had been loosened and the top buttons of his shirt undone. Black hair, the same sun-gilded hair that covered strong forearms, showed at his neck.

Gaby swallowed and passed her tongue over her lips. She noticed his attention go to her mouth . . . and his chest, his broad chest, with every muscle delineated beneath the perfectly fitted shirt, expanded with a deep breath.

She changed her mind. She'd *never, ever,* felt anything like this before. Her skin tingled. Somewhere deep inside her belly a burning contraction hit and sent a tense ache into her thighs.

At the instant when a bolt of warning finally sounded in her numbed brain — he smiled. A marvelous smile, lazily sexy and feral, that drove dimples into lean cheeks. The vague shadow of a beard darkened his jaw.

Gaby walked to the center of the shop.

The man transferred his hands from his hips to his pockets and approached until he stood only feet from her. There were chips of black in those deep blue eyes, and his lashes were thicker than any man's ought to be.

He'd stopped smiling.

"Is there something I can do to help you?" Gaby asked, all too aware of the crack in her husky voice.

A ghost of a smile showed strong, white teeth. "I'm sure there is."

Gaby nibbled her bottom lip and swallowed with difficulty. Any suggestiveness she felt in this man had to be imagined . . . didn't it?

He looked at her mouth again.

She wasn't imagining a thing. This was the sexiest man she had ever come within a mile of, and he was standing only grabbing distance away . . . staring straight at her mouth, her breasts, her hips. He was assessing her all the way to her bare, sandaled feet.

"Are you lost?" she asked, feeling inane and hot and afraid he'd leave . . . and equally as nervous that he'd stay.

"Lost?"

"Did you need directions?"

"No."

A faint scent of warm musk and clean skin almost closed her eyes. "How can I help you?"

Tipping his head to one side, he studied her all over again, starting at her toes and finishing at her eyes. "I'm not sure anymore. Not as sure as I was when I walked in here."

His voice was deep and warm, a voice that flowed along a woman's nerves like heated honey with a disguised bite.

Gaby breathed in deeply again — and saw his attention flicker away from her face.

He pulled a long, broad hand from his pocket and held it out. Gaby slipped her own graceful fingers into his palm and found herself held as surely as if he'd embraced her.

"Are you Gaby McGregor?"

She frowned. "Yes."

"I thought so. I'm Jacques Ledan."

2

Five minutes ago he'd have said he wasn't in the mood. Now he was definitely in the mood and, if he had to guess, he'd say the woman whose hand still rested in his and who showed no sign of wanting it to be anywhere else, was feeling more than a twinge of the same sexual charge that had just hit him.

"I thought . . ." Her eyes — green, shimmering eyes flecked with yellow, like those of a sleek cat — slid away toward the window of her shop. The black straw hat that she wore tipped forward over her brow could only be worn by a woman with such dramatic looks. "Two people just left. A Rita Nagel and . . . I thought that man was Jacques Ledan."

Jacques shook his head. "Rita's my assistant. The man with her is Bart Stanly. He's working on planning and development for my project in Goldstrike."

The cool hand was quickly withdrawn. "Yes. Your project."

So, Rita's instincts had probably been right.

There was less than enthusiasm here. "I understand Rita mentioned the work I'd like you to consider doing for me."

Gaby McGregor's full mouth turned down. "She mentioned it." A wonderful, sensual mouth. A mouth that would move so well beneath the lips and tongue of a man who was an expert in such matters.

Jacques stared into her eyes once more and met pure hostility. Bart was definitely no judge of reactions. "Overwhelmed," he'd insisted. Gaby McGregor was "bowled over" by the generous offer of work. Well, she wasn't, Jacques knew, but he was damned if he could begin to understand why. He'd noted a general air of sluggishness pervading Goldstrike every time he'd driven through on the way to his house in the foothills beyond.

"How much do you know about my plans, I wonder." Perhaps it was time to explain more to the locals. He'd hesitated to do so while so much was uncertain, but now everything was set to go.

The woman moved next to him and stared out of the window. "You intend to bring Goldstrike into the twentieth century. That's what your assistant told me." The brim of the hat shaded her face, cast rounded shadows beneath her high cheekbones. Her skin was smooth and pale with the faintest peachy blush on her cheeks.

"Rita has a somewhat . . . individual way

34

of putting things sometimes." No, Gaby McGregor was not delighted with whatever picture Rita had painted. "I've been coming through this valley for almost fifteen years now — since I was a teenager —"

"To your house. Everyone here knows about it."

Did everyone here also feel as hostile about the subject as Gaby McGregor did? "Have you seen La Place?"

She gave a short laugh. "La Place. No, I haven't seen it."

"You sound as if you've decided you wouldn't like it."

She looked at him and shrugged. "I'm never likely to see it, and it really doesn't matter whether or not I'd like it."

Jacques made no attempt to ignore the fact that the shrug had allowed the wide neck of a lacy red over-blouse to slip from an ivory shoulder. "I hope you will see it," he said with absolute honesty. "It's a beautiful house. You'd look good in it."

She blushed slightly and wonderfully and ran her tongue over her lips, leaving the skin moist . . . and driving the dart of desire ever more sharply into the part of him that made his pants suddenly too tight.

"Rita spoke to me from the phone in the limo. Since I was coming through town, anyway, I decided to stop and talk to you myself." There was some other element here, something completely different from anything he remembered feeling. He was probably reacting to the unusual sensation that he was being confronted by a will as strong as his own. "Tell me what concerns you. There is something?"

The breath she drew raised her full breasts again. Through the loose, lacy blouse he could see that she wore a strapless red top. Between the top and the waist of slim pants there was the suggestion of slim, bare midriff.

He checked her left hand. No rings. What did a single woman, one who looked and sounded like Gaby McGregor, do for diversion in a sleepy town several hours' drive from civilization?

One thing she didn't do was talk a lot.

"Isn't it pretty quiet here?"

"In Goldstrike, you mean?"

He could watch that mouth form words for a very long time. "Yes, in Goldstrike. Don't you get bored?" Now he sounded as if he was coming on to her.

"I never get bored."

Strike one. He looked around the shop. To his inexpert eye her merchandise appeared completely out of place for the area. "You make hats." It could be that she'd bought all this stuff somewhere just to use for decoration.

He caught Gaby's eye and winced. "Did I

say something wrong?" She was staring at him with something close to green hatred.

"Didn't you send Rita here because you knew I 'made' hats, as you put it?"

"Yes." Realization dawned. She felt threatened by him. "I really did mean that I'd like you to fill an order for me. I don't usually deal with these things myself, but —"

"Rita told me how carefully you avoid the little people."

"As I was saying. I usually leave the people I hire to deal with such matters. Goldstrike is special to me. I want to be personally involved." He would only take just so much unwarranted antagonism. "Do you feel threatened?"

She stared. "Threatened?"

"By me."

Her laugh made his spine tingle. "Men don't frighten me, Mr. Ledan."

"I didn't mean physically."

"Neither did I."

Jacques walked behind her and stood, looking down at her neck. "You're hostile." Let her decide what to do next.

"Am I?"

"I think so. I came here to be pleasant. You're giving me the brush-off and I want to know why."

"You're imagining things."

"I don't think so." His height had many advantages, not the least of which was his vantage point on her now. Her neck was smooth and slender, a dramatic contrast to the heavy braid of black hair that fell to the middle of her back. And between the pale swell of her breasts lay deep and enticing cleavage. "I have no intention of doing anything that won't be a benefit to the people of this town . . . to you. Do you think you could help me make that understood?"

"What exactly are you proposing that I make understood?"

He bent a little to see the side of her face. "That I don't intend to take business away from them. You do know that? I certainly don't intend to undermine your business, Gaby." Not that he could imagine her having any business in Goldstrike.

"I thought your business was candy, Mr. Ledan. Do you make hats, too?"

He smiled. "Very amusing. I think you know what I mean."

Gaby looked up at him and his breath stuck in his throat. She was beautiful — completely unexpectedly and absolutely gorgeous.

"Could we get together, Gaby? Maybe for dinner at the house?"

Her arched brows rose. "I doubt it."

Only with difficulty did he stop himself from touching her. "Think about it and I'll get back to you." What I'd like to do is explain exactly what I have in mind for this town. It's evident from our first direct contacts that some people may have the wrong impression. You could help me change that."

"I really don't think so."

Didn't think so, or didn't want to think so? "What I've observed in the past few years — since I've spent more time at La Place — is the almost total absence of young people here. They're moving out, and who can blame them? There has to be something for them to do, something to get excited about. With an infusion of money into the area and opportunities for good-paying jobs, the younger generation will stop leaving, and some who have already left will come back."

Gaby walked away. When she reached a desk on one side of the shop, she faced him. "Is that the carrot you intend to hang in front of us?"

"Why —" He advanced, then stopped. This lady was sending mixed signals. Her words said she didn't trust him and didn't want anything to do with him — something he couldn't begin to figure out. Her body language spelled a very different message. She wasn't any more unaffected by their meeting than he was. "Revitalizing Goldstrike is my aim. I do plan to lure the younger generation back — or encourage them to stay, whichever is appropriate. And I intend to bring new people into the area. Isn't that already understood here?"

"What's understood is that you have plans to open a resort hotel and buy up any suitable properties for shops."

He nodded. "That's part of it."

"And you're trying to design some sort of displays with *leprechauns*."

"Roughly." He narrowed his eyes. "Do you know everyone around here?"

"Yes, I do."

"Are they worried about what may happen?" He'd never intended to do anything but help. All that would be necessary would be to gain the people's confidence.

Gaby McGregor wasn't saying anything.

"Rita said you were thinking over the idea of making caps for us."

Still she didn't speak.

"She told you we'd have to move to a bigger outfit when we need to produce in large numbers?"

Gaby averted her face.

"Look, it won't be the end of the world. When that happens I'm sure arrangements could be made for you to have the exclusive sales outlet for the caps here."

She made a strangled noise.

Damn. "Everything will work out for the best. Leave it to me."

"Will you excuse me?" She turned her brilliant eyes on him once more.

What could he say? "Of course. But I'm not giving up on that chat."

"You should."

In the soft afternoon sunlight streaming through the window, she was cast in gold tints. Slender, yet all woman, Gaby McGregor sent a clear message to Jacques, one admittedly received most strongly by his hormones, but not entirely so. She was sharp and sexy and he would want to find out just how sexy.

He remembered what he'd been heading into town to do and suppressed a smile. "We're bound to be seeing each other frequently, anyway."

"Why?" she asked baldly, planting her feet apart.

"Oh, because I've decided I need to have an office in town during the heavy planning phase. It's always best to be in the middle of things where business is concerned." Not that he'd ever been in the middle of the business he'd headed, up till now. Ledan's clicked along very nicely with little more than his presence at board meetings and his signature on a never-ending heap of dotted lines. "Yes, I'll be in Goldstrike a good deal of the time in the months to come."

"I'm always very busy," Gaby said. "I don't get around town much."

Jacques made a decision, one of the few he'd ever made in quite such a hurry. "If I'm

41

not mistaken, you won't have to get around to see me." He pulled out the list he'd been carrying in his shirt pocket and pretended to study it. "I'm . . . You're not going to believe this, but unless you're planning to move your business —"

"I'm *not*."

"Good." He approached the door. "You do rent this space from a Mr. Shaw?"

"Yes." Her face was tight.

"This really is a coincidence. I made en-quiries about empty spaces that might be available in Goldstrike. But maybe you al-ready knew that?"

She nodded.

"Yes, of course you did. We discovered this building had unoccupied space upstairs. Bart was saying he thought it would convert into a great suite of offices. I've decided I agree with him, so you'll be seeing a lot of me." He smiled his most charming smile. "I hope you'll be as happy about that as I am."

3

Sunday mornings wouldn't be the same without breakfast at Sis's. Gaby propped her elbows on the brown Formica-topped table, cradled her thick, yellow coffee mug in both hands and pretended not to see Mae hide most of her egg beneath a piece of toast.

The rush had thinned. In addition to Gaby and Mae, a group of farmers hunched in a back booth were the only remaining patrons. Warm maple syrup, crispy bacon and fresh-brewed coffee were the scents of the moment.

"What d'you feel like doing today?" Gaby asked, already anticipating the response.

"Gonna help Sis. She says I can put the apples in the pies." Mae's current ambition was to run a diner "just like Sis's," which the girl considered to be the hub of everything exciting that happened in Goldstrike.

"Maybe you should ask if it's all right with me, Mae."

"You always say it's all right."

Gaby looked down at Mae's shiny black ponytail and the soft curve of her seven-year-old cheek. Life was mostly very wonderful. "I guess I do." She gave the ponytail a gentle tug. "Don't get in the way. And call me when Sis is tired of you."

The door opened to admit Sophie Byler, elderly but spry and still exuding the all-seeing alertness of a small-town school-teacher — which was exactly what she'd been before she retired.

"Morning, Sis." Sophie nodded curtly at the tall, stately owner of the diner and headed for Gaby's booth. "Char tells me you had a few visitors yesterday." She slid in to sit opposite Gaby and Mae.

"It's as bad as you said it was, Sophie," Gaby said. "Probably worse. Did Char give you the scoop about mining exhibits and leprechauns?"

Sophie shuddered. "We aren't taking it lying down. We aren't taking it at all. We've got some history to preserve here. Maybe it's not significant to the rest of the world, but it is to us . . . and to our children."

The school had closed a couple of years after Sophie, already in her late sixties then, had decided to spend her days pleasing only herself — which meant she became the self-appointed guardian of Goldstrike's affairs. And since then the children had been bussed many miles for their education. Sophie had never stopped talking to the town's young-sters about their heritage, or trying to find a way to have them stay closer to home for their studies.

"Ledan made a point of how the younger generation moves on as soon as they can," Gaby said morosely. "Great revelation — they need jobs and incentive and we don't have a whole lot of either around here."

Sophie, her white hair wound into its customary severe knot at her nape, rested a gnarled hand on Gaby's forearm. "We aren't beaten. Six years ago you brought something special to this town. What we should be looking for are more ways to get people like you interested, people who won't want to change things. You liked the place enough to decide to run a business here that most folks would have taken to a big city. And it works just fine, doesn't it?"

Gaby nodded. "There's no denying we need much more than I'm doing if there's going to be a permanent fix."

"Don't tell me you're giving up on us, too, girl."

"I'm not giving up. Just trying to be realistic. Ledan's got what it takes to be very persuasive." And totally unforgettable. She tamped down that thought. "He already talked — or had one of his people talk the Bartletts into selling."

Sophie turned down her mouth, sending ripples of wrinkles across her thin, pink skin. "Abe Bartlett's spineless. Forget him. Put your mind to how we can get more people like you to move out here."

"Easier said than — Mae, sit still."

"I just wanna go look out the window."

The pattern was predictable. Mae had a fascination with what the locals called The Table; a table in the window, covered with an orange vinyl cloth and set for three diners. Three chairs were tipped up at those place settings.

"You can look out of the window from here," Gaby said. "You know what happened the last time you sat at The Table."

Mae wiggled but said nothing.

"Sis didn't speak to you for a week, and she wouldn't let you help for another week after that."

The Table was kept exclusively for Sis's three silent brothers, and it was understood that no one else ever sat there. It was said to have the best view in the place. That was true: a view of the corner gas station with a tiny sliver of distant mountain — if you pressed your nose to the glass.

Sophie took a fork and moved aside Mae's slice of toast, revealing the congealed remnants of a sunny-side up fried egg. "Concentrate on finishing the good food your mother's paying for," she said severely. "You'll never do well in school if you don't eat properly. And you're too thin."

Mae sighed and waited until Sophie looked

at Gaby again before performing the egg's burial once more.

"The committee against Ledan is coming along nicely," Sophie said. "Artie and Freda are on board. And Barney — though sometimes I wish that gaudy hacienda of his would just disappear. Caleb at the gas station — and his wife, of course. And every one of them is taking a section of the town and visiting people personally. I'm planning a meeting for two weeks from tonight in the Women's Auxiliary Hall."

"This is going to be a tough fight." Gaby looked up as Sis approached with fresh coffee. Sis was almost as silent as her brothers and refilled Gaby's mug without a word. She set down a second mug for Sophie and retreated. "Ledan's opening an office above my place."

"What!"

"Mommy says it isn't nice to say *what,*" Mae said pompously. "You're supposed to say excuse me, or I beg your pardon."

Sophie ignored her. "Ledan's going to use that empty space up there? Isn't it just an old storage area?"

"He says it's going to be renovated." She lifted her loose hair from her neck. "Imagine the noise and mess that's going to mean."

"What's he like?"

Gaby met the other woman's light eyes, and her mind immediately slid away, back to yesterday and the moment when Jacques Ledan had faced her in the shop. Today, as then, her legs felt weak and achy. Just what she needed, a sexy rush over a man who didn't know she was alive other than as a maker of baseball caps! "It'll be a cold day in hell," she muttered.

"I beg your pardon?" Sophie's eyes widened.

Gaby flapped a hand. "Talking to myself. He told me how he wants to use all the little people in Goldstrike. Give them jobs to make them feel included. My job was supposed to be making baseball caps with dumb logos on the front."

Now Sophie really stared. "Doesn't he know what you do?" she whispered, almost reverently.

Gaby grimaced. "Oh, sure. I *make* hats. Why wouldn't I be delighted to make hundreds of caps with GFTG in Goldstrike on the front . . . in my little *factory*."

Before Sophie could do more than start to respond, the door opened once more and a woman's strident voice announced, "Will you look at this. You didn't tell me it was like this, Bart. Jacques, did he tell you?"

"No. But I've driven by many times."

Gaby ducked her head and scooted lower in the seat. The last thing she wanted was another eye-to-eye confrontation with Jacques

Ledan, not until she'd decided what her next move would be.

"Is it them?" Sophie croaked.

"Mmm."

"What's the matter, Mom?"

Gaby aimed a warning frown at Mae, who had taken her burial one stage further and was squishing down the toast with the back of her fork. The child wrinkled her nose and kept quiet.

"Ma'am," Rita said loudly. "Excuse me, ma'am."

Sis grunted.

"Is the floor dry over here now?"

"Weren't wet," Sis said and continued wiping the counter.

Clattering followed and Gaby dared a peek toward the window. Rita was pulling the chairs away from The Table. "Let's sit here. More light. I want to show you some of the figures the accountants gave me."

The three sat around The Table.

"I saw those two parties you mentioned and they're agreeable," Bart Stanly said. "All we need is the old guy . . . Damned if I remember his name. The one to the north. That'll give us all the space we need to start with."

"I don't want any hitches now," Jacques Ledan said, his voice deeper than Stanly's and with that quality Gaby had noticed yesterday: soft, yet clear and with a hint of gravel that singed her nerves.

"They're sitting at The Table, Mommy," Mae said. "Sis is getting real mad. Look."

Sis being *real mad* meant her plump face turned red and she stood like a statue with her arms crossed.

"Mommy," Mae hissed. "If she stays mad I won't get to help make pies!"

Sophie, clearly unable to resist any longer, craned to see the trio in the window. Returning her attention to Gaby, she asked, "Is that *really* them?"

"Uh-huh."

"And Ledan's the dark one." She sniffed. "French. You can see that."

"His grandfather was French," Gaby said, keeping her voice low although Rita and Bart were too busy vying for Ledan's attention to be aware of anyone else. "Take it from me. This one's all-American entrepreneur."

"Been investigating?" Sophie asked. Her mouth had thinned to a pale line.

"I had a friend in Los Angeles make some enquiries. The Ledans started making candy in a small way in France. Then the grandfather came to the States and began building the business here. The son built a whole lot more. Four years ago he retired to the south of France, leaving his son, the original Ledan's grandson — Jacques — to run things. They're big in Europe as well as the States."

"So what does he want with us?" Sophie asked, hardly moving her lips.

"Who knows?" Gaby responded. "Either he's bored or he's greedy. Probably some of both."

"Mom, Sis looks funny."

"I'll see to it," Sophie said, getting up. She marched to the counter, picked up menus and took them to Ledan and the dynamic duo. "Are you sure you want to sit here?" she asked. "Sun gets hot through the window."

Gaby looked down into her cup and waited.

"We're fine," Rita said. "I'll have decaffeinated. Regular for you two, right?"

A chorus of masculine grunts followed.

Gaby suppressed a grin. The arrogant ignorance of these people was amusing — almost.

Sophie passed the booth, brows raised almost to her hairline, walked behind the counter and picked up two coffee carafes. Sis continued to stand like a large, irritable statue. Gaby could see her lips moving but couldn't hear a word she might be saying.

"You sure you wouldn't like a different table?" Sophie asked and Gaby heard coffee splashing into mugs. "It's a whole lot more private in a booth."

"We like this table," Rita said. "How long have you lived here?"

"Seventy-five years," Sophie said promptly.

"My," Rita said, her voice patronizingly sweet. "And still waiting tables. That's really wonderful."

God help Jacques Ledan. Gaby bent her face and rested her brow on a fist to hide her grin. Sophie Byler wasn't an enemy she'd like to have, and she had a hunch Mr. Ledan wasn't going to enjoy it, either.

The squish, squish of rubber-soled shoes preceded the arrival of Sis who did what Gaby had never known her to do before — she sat down in the booth. Her face had passed through red and arrived at purple.

Gaby reached for the woman's crossed arms and squeezed a broad wrist. "Don't be upset," she whispered. "They're strangers."

"Chairs was tipped," Sis mumbled. "Chairs is always tipped."

Sophie had appropriated the order pad and was standing at Bart Stanly's elbow, pencil poised. "Oatmeal's great," she said. "Though there's some would say it's an acquired taste if you don't like it real thin. Chicken gizzard and pig's heart fry goes down well with a mess of lima beans and bread fried in bacon grease to wipe it up with. Fill you up, let me tell you. Won't need no dinner."

Sis's mouth fell open.

Mae giggled.

"Won't *want* dinner, or any other meal for a while," Gaby said under her breath. Sophie was nothing if not inventive.

"We'll stick with the coffee," Bart said.

Gaby glanced up . . . directly into those blue eyes she was never going to forget. Ledan became still — still in the way that had made the air seem breathless the previous afternoon. He smiled, and Gaby's lips parted before she looked away. The man spelled danger of the worst kind, the kind that attacked the body and maybe the heart and then moved in for the kill.

Sophie returned and sat beside Sis. There was nothing to say, and Gaby studied her hands.

"This place is *cute!*" Rita said. "I had no idea there were still places like this around. It's like something out of a Western movie, right down to the little-old-grandma waitress."

Mae giggled again and Gaby had to peek at Sophie. Thunderous didn't do her expression justice.

War was declared.

"I told you the town was old," Jacques said. He sounded distracted and Gaby was certain that if she looked at him, he'd be looking right back. "That's the point. It hasn't changed since gold prospecting days. Not significantly. If it isn't given a chance it's going to disappear."

"We should try to keep this diner as it is," Bart said. "It's going to be important to play up the old-world, forgotten stuff. People are going to eat up a chance to take a look at primitive places like this."

Gaby listened closely. The more she knew about Ledan's plans, the better. She had to sit tight and not show her hand too soon, or else fighting him would be even harder.

"The teen club is what interests me," Jacques said. "What I said about the young people isn't going to change unless we can get them hooked into liking where they live, and soon. With the right facility, the local kids will mingle with the tourist teens. A little excitement's all we need to make more of them want to stay. Particularly if they see there are going to be jobs for them here, too."

A teen club sounded like a great idea. And the jobs. But Gaby already knew they were all going to hate the idea when Ledan got through with them.

"Bart's got a great plan, haven't you?" Rita said, sounding blissful. "Tell Jacques what you told me this morning."

"It's simple really," Bart said. "The old schoolhouse is the perfect spot for a teen club. There's a kind of underlying kick to the idea of using a place that used to be a follow-the-rules stronghold. Think of it. Teenagers cutting up on hallowed ground as it were."

Gaby met Sophie's cold eyes and the old woman shook her head slowly.

Rita gave an enthusiastic whoop. "Bart says the hall's small but for a start it'll work for dancing. We can add something that looks like a gymnasium later — in conjunction with the resort."

"Yeah," Bart said. "There's a stage in the hall for the DJ. Throw in the strobe lights and a great sound system and you'll have kids coming from miles around."

"The school's beside a trailer park," Jacques said. "What about the noise —"

"We'll move the park. No sweat." Bart laughed. "Everything's got a price. I've already started getting bids for the video concessions. We'll turn the corridors into video arcades. This is going to be dynamite, Jacques. The farther in I get, the more excited I am. Give me six months and you won't recognize this town."

Sis's hand went to her mouth.

"It's okay," Gaby said, not at all certain anything would ever be okay around here again, but determined not to give up without a fight. "Stay put and don't say a word. Please look after Mae until I get back."

She left the booth and walked the length of the diner — with Ledan's eyes on her every step of the way. "Excuse me —" she smiled at him "— but I wonder if I could speak with you privately."

Without waiting for his answer, Gaby left the restaurant. When the door clicked shut,

Ledan was already at her shoulder.

She faced him. "I'm sorry to take you away from your friends."

"I'm glad you did. And they're my employees, not my friends."

Gaby wondered what kind of people he would count as friends. "Nevertheless, I hope you'll excuse me for breaking in."

"You can break in on me anytime you like."

The slow warming of her blood started again. "I only wanted to talk to you for a few minutes — about your plans here. Would it be appropriate for me to do that?" Charm and manners could often achieve what anger would make impossible.

He regarded her with what felt like intense intimacy. His concentration on her mouth sent her tongue nervously over her lips and she saw his sharp intake of breath.

"I'd like to show you something," he said abruptly, taking her elbow. He smiled down into her face. "Can I steal you away for a little while?"

Her skin tingled where he touched her. "For a little while," she agreed, while common sense told her that this man was much too persuasive for safe company.

The dusty green Jeep stood at the curb with a silver Porsche parked behind. Ledan shepherded Gaby to the Jeep and helped her in.

When he sat beside her he smiled, and in

the sunlight his eyes were tropical sea lapis, the color of deep water over a coral reef.

"What about your . . . the others?"

"They're Porsche people." He hooked a thumb over his shoulder. "That's Bart's. They won't wait for me."

With that, he drove away, heading out of town to the north. "I shouldn't be gone too long," Gaby said. This was the way he must come when he went to La Place. What a name for a house!

"We aren't going far," Ledan said.

About ten miles out of town he took a sharp left turn down a dirt track leading to one of the farms. Gaby knew it was owned by a family named Odle who kept to themselves.

Once through a sagging wooden gate propped open with a pile of old tires, Ledan drove straight toward the shabby clapboard farmhouse but skirted the building and continued through groves of stripped peach trees.

Dust sprayed from beneath the Jeep's wide tires and the smell of fallen fruit and warm dirt hung heavy in the air.

At last, when there was nothing in sight but acres of trees and crisp brown grass with a crystal-blue sky stretching to the mountains, Ledan parked and walked around to Gaby's side.

"Let me." Before she could climb out, his

hands closed on her waist and he lifted her effortlessly down until they stood, toe to toe.

"Thank you, Mr. Ledan." Her hands rested on flexed biceps.

"Jacques." His throat was deeply tanned against the open collar of his khaki shirt.

"Jacques."

Beneath his fingers her gauze dress was too thin, too flimsy a shield between his skin and hers. His grip on her waist tightened slightly. "Is this private enough, Gaby?"

She started. He made a new sound of her name, something oddly foreign and exotic.

He smiled again. "You did say you wanted to talk to me privately."

"And you asked if you could steal me away for a while."

"And I have, haven't I?" The tilt of his head, the parting of his lips to show such even, white teeth, sent her stomach plunging.

Gaby stepped away. "You certainly have." She walked farther from him up the slight incline of the orchard. The trees stretched endlessly on all sides.

Jacques fell in beside her. "You aren't from Goldstrike — not originally?"

"No. I've lived here for six years, though, and it's the only home I ever want from now on."

"Really?" he sounded amazed.

"Really. Not everyone wants to race on the fast track. Some of us can hardly wait to get off."

He strolled, a stride to every two or three of Gaby's steps. "Were you ever on the fast track?"

She smiled to herself. "Too fast for me." And that was all she'd volunteer.

"What did you want to talk to me about?"

They'd reached a knoll bisected by a leaning wire fence that meant another farmer's land lay on the other side. Gaby thought carefully before she said, "I wanted to ask you about your plans for Goldstrike. You can refuse to tell me, of course."

"Ask me anything." He braced a straight arm against a tree and looked out over the land rolling away before them.

Gaby wiped her damp palms on her skirt. She was grateful for the breeze that stirred her hair and cooled her skin — though not nearly enough. "You, er, you really ought to wear a hat more," she said in a rush.

He glanced back at her. "Why?"

"Too much sun isn't good for you." This was a mistake. She hadn't thought through what she needed to say, and experience had taught her that acting first and thinking second rarely worked out too well.

"I don't wear hats."

"You should. They'd suit you." She felt sick.

Jacques grinned. "I'll take that as a compliment, but I still don't wear hats. What did you want to ask me?"

A slow, calm approach would be best. An oblique attack. "Are you married?" *Wonderful!*

"No." He appeared unmoved. "Are you?"

"No."

"I'm glad to hear that."

Gaby looked at her bare toes and dusty beige sandals. Now he must think she was personally interested in him.

"You're beautiful, Gaby. But I expect you know that."

The ground felt as if it was slipping away. "Your grandfather started Ledan's, didn't he?" Now he'd figure out she'd been digging up his background.

"Yes. He came from France with a few old family recipes and more hopes and ambitions than you can imagine — and a great big heart. Almost no money, though." He laughed. "My father took over about twenty years ago and passed the reins to me five years ago."

Gaby raised her shoulders.

"My parents live in the south of France now. My grandfather died only ten years ago. D'you know what his last words were to me?"

"No." She wanted to watch his face, loved watching his face.

"He said, 'One day you'll meet your nemesis, Jacques.' And then he went to sleep. He was ninety-seven. Guess what he meant by that?"

Gaby chafed her arms and shook her head. "I don't know."

"I didn't think you would. Maybe I'll tell you one day." He ran a finger from her shoulder to her elbow and rubbed a fold of the loose dress between finger and thumb. "You look good in this. It touches all the right places."

She felt a blush speed up her neck.

"Particularly when the breeze blows it against your legs . . . and the rest of you." His eyes passed boldly over her before he turned back to the landscape.

For the first time in longer than she could remember, a raw surge of heat flashed in her breasts and all the way to her knees. He was setting out to confuse her and succeeding masterfully.

Gaby wrapped her arms around her ribs and drew herself up. "I heard some of what you said at Sis's."

"Did you?"

"Yes. Goldstrike doesn't want what you're peddling." Her heart pounded.

"Doesn't it?"

"No. These people like the way of life they lead. They're simple and kind . . . like this land. They don't need discos and — and strobe lights and mining displays and resorts. They don't —"

"They do need them. And they will want them. If something doesn't happen around here there won't be a Goldstrike. Where will all these simple, kind people be then?"

"It won't happen. I —"

"*You* are a very special, one-of-a-kind woman. But you don't know what you're talking about. Keep on being special. Especially around me. But leave business to business people."

She made fists and had to quell an urge to pummel him with them. "What do you think I . . . Scratch that. I know what you think I am. *Who* do you think *you* are?"

"I'm Jacques Ledan and I've been driving through Goldstrike since I was a kid. My best times have been right here. I'm a Californian, Gaby. I was born in this state. Its history is important to me — preserving the past for future generations. The pioneer culture that founded places like Goldstrike, molded me."

"But it didn't make you want it for what it is, did it? You want to change it and make a lot of money in the process."

"I want to help it stay alive." He turned and rested his back on the tree. His eyes were blue ice now. "Sure there are going to be dissenters, but they'll be a minority and they'll dissent out of pride."

She took an involuntary step toward him. "What's wrong with a little pride? It makes people strong and focused."

"What's the point of being strong and focused while what little you have falls down around you?"

"They won't be happy, Jacques." The tears of passion that sprang into her eyes weren't welcome. "You're going to take away their identity."

"I'm going to give them a way to preserve it. You see this land we're standing on?"

"Yes." Gaby hugged herself tighter.

"I've bought this farm. And the one behind me. And I intend to get one or two more in the same block. This is going to become a theme park that people will come to from all over the country — damn it, from all over the world."

Gaby raised a hand to her mouth, but Jacques caught her wrist.

"People resist change," Jacques said. "But when they get used to it, they love what it can do for them. I'm going to find a way to bring water in here. There'll be a huge waterslide area — bigger than anything like it anywhere. When people are deciding where to vacation, they'll be considering going for the gold in Goldstrike. This isn't a tacky joke. *This is big business.* And we're all going to benefit from it."

Gaby drew in a breath that burned. "You're going to turn our little town into another resort area? I got out of Los Angeles because I wanted some peace. Everyone who chooses to stay here wants peace."

"According to you."

With her free hand she grabbed his shirt. "I . . . I . . ."

She never finished the thought or the sentence. Jacques yanked her against him and his mouth came down on hers. His lips were warm and firm and supple. His eyes closed and he wrapped her in big, strong arms from which she'd only escape when he chose to let her go. The kiss was forceful, wild and possessive. Gaby's legs weakened and her grip on his shirt became the anchor that stopped her from falling.

Jacques groaned and his hands slid down to cross over her bottom. Spreading his legs, he pressed her hips into his pelvis. He was hard. And the fit was right.

This kiss softened to a nipping, nuzzling, searing thing that rocked Gaby's face from side to side. She ran her palms up his chest and around his neck until she could tangle her fingers in his hair.

She smelled his clean scent, felt his hard chest crushing her breasts and wanted to feel his hands there — his lips.

"Gaby," he whispered, kissing her cheek, her closed eyes, her ear. "Gaby, Gaby." Holding her ever more strongly against his arousal, he pushed his fingers through her hair and returned to her mouth.

He sucked her lower lip gently between his

teeth, then thrust his tongue deeply into her mouth.

His hand shifted from her hair, smoothed her shoulder, slipped to cover and knead her breast. In an instant he'd eased down her low neckline and found a straining nipple. Pinching lightly, rolling, he turned her legs to useless things and her womb to a molten place that drove her hips against him again and again.

Farther down he shifted the loose bodice, far enough to free her naked breasts.

"Oh, my God!" Panting, pushing him away, pushing back her hair, Gaby tore herself from him. "What do you think you're doing?"

He took his hands from her, held out his palms. His chest rose and fell with great, dragging breaths. "I'm doing exactly what you know I'm doing." Desire made his eyes brilliant, the lines of his face rigid. "*We're* doing exactly what we know we're doing. Sometimes these things are meant to happen. This is one of those times."

"No. No." Hitching at her dress she backed away. "Never. Not to me. This doesn't happen to me."

"This?" He shrugged away from the tree and winced.

Gaby's eyes went to his pants and she looked quickly away. What had happened to him wasn't going away. Her own desire throbbed in every vein. And it was nothing but lust.

"Gaby. What do you mean by *this?*"

"Casual encounters." She shook her head violently. "I asked you to talk to me about . . . professional matters. Business was what I had in mind."

He smiled, the slow, incredibly sensual smile that made her throat feel entirely closed. "There's no reason to allow business to infringe on . . . other things."

She stared. "Take me back, please." This man was telling her that there was no reason to allow major differences in every other area to interfere with the possibility of great sex. Gaby managed to swallow. If what had happened was a barometer, sex with Jacques Ledan would be unbelievably great. "I want to go back."

"Fine, I'll take you. But don't think this is a closed subject. And I'm not talking about *business.*"

Gaby started walking. "We are on opposite sides in a war."

"Not between us. Not unless you call what just happened some sort of battle." He caught up easily and slipped an arm around her waist, jerked her back when she tried to escape him. "That kind of battle I'll engage in any day. As many times a day as I can persuade you to be with me."

"There won't be other times. This won't —

what happened won't happen again."

He spread his hand over her ribcage until his thumb could range back and forth across the soft underside of her breast. "It's going to happen, Gaby," he said softly and laughed. "It's going to happen again and again."

"No!"

"Yes." He swung her easily around to face him. "Right now I'll do what you want. I'll take you back to Goldstrike and safety. But you're never going to be safe again. Not from me."

4

Another wad of aluminum foil zipped past Jacques, hit sagging pink insulation and dropped to the base of an exposed wall stud.

Jacques rounded on Bart and said, "Enough with the missiles," in a low voice. The three workmen who wandered the length of the unfinished space, tapping, banging and muttering, were unlikely to hear, anyway.

Bart Stanly, slouched in a discarded metal lawn chair with no cushions, began rolling another piece of foil from a very old TV dinner cover. "We're wasting time in this dump." He formed the tarnished ball deliberately between his palms. "You don't need an office downtown. Not that you can say this burg has a downtown."

"I do need it," Jacques said shortly. "Damn, it's hot up here." He undid several buttons on his khaki shirt.

"Yup." Bart rolled and rolled the foil while his eyes lost focus. "And it's going to stay hot up here. Heat rises, in case you haven't noticed. What's wrong with the office at La Place?"

"The office at La Place is there, not here. That's what's wrong with it." No way would he give Bart even an inkling of the real reason for turning this musty-smelling second story into his project headquarters. "The people around here are bound to react better to someone who's more accessible."

"You won't be dealing with the people, Jacques. Rita and I will. That's the arrangement."

"*Was* the arrangement," he corrected. "I've changed my mind. If they're going to stop viewing me as some outsider whose only interest is in exploiting them, I'm going to have to gain their trust."

"And you think this —" Bart indicated dusty beams, bare wooden floorboards, trailing electrical wires and the detritus of previous inhabitants "— this is somehow going to make them trust you? Why? Because you decide to put a desk into a slum?"

Bart could be damned obtuse. Sometimes Jacques wondered why he put up with the man. He wouldn't if Bart hadn't already proved himself very capable. "This slum, as you call it, is going to be renovated. Give it a week and you won't recognize the place."

Evidently the workmen heard the word *week*. Three pairs of eyes riveted on Jacques.

"A week, Mr. Ledan?" Cal Simms, local contractor, wiped scarred hands on his white

69

overalls and ambled up. "I thought you said we were going to put up wallboard and complete all the finishing."

"You are," Jacques said patiently. "Full bathroom. Kitchen. Bedroom. Sitting room incorporated with the office space."

Air hissed between Bart's teeth. Jacques ignored him.

Cal removed his sweat-stained white cap and scratched his balding scalp. "Months of work there, Mr. Ledan. Months."

Jacques moved to a window overlooking the back of the building. "Two weeks, max," he said with finality. "I'm going to tell you what goes where and you're going to see everything gets there." He almost smiled at Cal's bewildered expression. "Pull in as many extra people as you need. Let me know the specs and who you use for supplies. Bart here will deal with anyone who doesn't think they can deliver on time — on time being in the next few days."

Cal's cohorts hovered in the background casting surreptitious glances at one another.

"This is all gonna cost." Cal frowned and shook his head. "We could do a nice job of cleaning up in here. Put in a john, burner for coffee . . . refrigerator for beer. Ain't like you got any long-term plans. Murphy bed, maybe —"

"I've got long-term plans," Jacques interrupted. Below the window was a roof. In that roof, a large skylight, cranked open to catch the breeze, reflected rays of afternoon sunshine. "And money isn't an issue. Best of everything." Directly in his line of vision, in the room revealed through the skylight, sat Gaby McGregor. "Yeah. I may be around a long, long time."

"We could be talkin' thousands —"

"We *are* talking thousands. Many thousands. Don't cut any corners." Gaby, her head bent over whatever she was sketching at a workbench, had drawn her hair up into a soft chignon at her crown. From his vantage point, Jacques saw the way a soft, white cotton shirt clung to . . . "This area by the window will be fine as an office space. Desk there." He hooked a thumb over his shoulder. The shirt clung to her full breasts, and Jacques had no difficulty visualizing what he couldn't actually see.

"It's going to take time, Mr. Ledan. Rome wasn't built in —"

"We're not building Rome," Jacques told Cal. "Just a suite." Pieces of Gaby's long, silky black hair had slipped from the chignon to rest on pale, smooth skin. He'd pushed his luck yesterday. Not that what had happened had been planned — not entirely. "Get the measurements down. My architect will be along shortly to draw something up."

Cal withdrew and the banging resumed.

Before the day was out, Jacques intended to

pursue what he'd begun with Gaby — at a more leisurely pace, if necessary.

"Ah." Bart had left his chair and come to stand at Jacques's shoulder. "I begin to understand. We're creating a lair and the prospective prey is in sight."

Jacques glanced back at Bart. "What the hell are you driveling about?"

"A little local diversion." Bart nodded toward the window. "I wouldn't have thought country girls were your style, but I guess there's not a whole lot to choose from around here."

Slowly Jacques looked from Bart's downcast eyes to Gaby. He wasn't sure exactly what he was feeling, but it wasn't pleasant.

Bart stepped closer. "Uh-huh. Maybe she's not bad by anyone's standards. Great face. I thought so the other day. And great —"

"That's enough."

"Hey!" Bart slapped his back. "Lighten up. You've been working too hard on this project. You know what all work and no play does to a guy. How long is it since you had some female company?"

"Drop it."

Bart held up his hands. "Okay, okay. I get the message. It's definitely been too long. But you'd better watch it with the little hayseed."

Jacques turned from the window and crossed his arms. "Okay, Bart, you've got my full attention. What d'you mean by that crack?"

"Oh, nothing much." An eloquent shrug lifted the shoulders of Bart's handmade, gray silk shirt. "Only that messing around with the local talent might not be such a great idea."

Jacques raised his chin. An unaccustomed shaft of annoyance straightened his spine. "I don't think I like what you're implying. Gaby McGregor isn't —" What exactly *wasn't* she? He liked her, that much he knew. And maybe he could come to more than like her, much more. "Gaby McGregor isn't the type of woman you refer to as *local talent*."

"Whatever you say." Bart laughed. "But I am the one who's supposed to work on making sure your image is snowy white in this town."

"My image is just fine," Jacques said through his teeth.

"Yeah. Sure." Bart studied his fingernails. "It's fine as long as no one looks at it too deeply. Turn over the surface and you're going to expose a one-hundred-percent playboy image."

"Talk," Jacques said explosively. "Just talk."

"Rich men gather reputations for high living whether they deserve to or not. And you have been known to do your part in that area. I know —" Bart held up a hand to stop Jacques's retort "— I know you've been a good boy for a long time. But once the story

73

of your efforts here hits the news, how long do you think it'll take the tabloids to dig up some juicy history?"

"If they do, it'll be just that. History."

"The way they use it, it won't sound like history." Bart reached for the briefcase he'd dropped on the floor. "I'd better get on with it. I'm meeting Rita at that greasy-spoon café."

"No one can invent what isn't true," Jacques said, but Bart's implication niggled.

"Can't they?" Bart headed for the stairs. "You know better than that. And Ms. McGregor seems to be the heroine in these parts. Almost a guru. Better keep your hands off if you don't want to get run out of town."

Before Jacques could reply, Bart clattered down the open staircase.

The mumbling group of workmen had congregated in a far corner where one of them jotted on dog-eared paper.

Jacques turned back to the window. She was still there. He wasn't sure when it had happened. Not the exact instant. But somewhere in the few days since he'd met Gaby McGregor, he'd made a discovery that excited his reportedly jaded core — and other parts of him. Collecting rare items had always been his passion. Gaby McGregor was a unique find — and he had to have her.

"Barney said it's all going to do the town a heap of good." Shirley, one of Gaby's first recruits to her work force, steamed pieces of purple felt, shaping them with deft fingers. "He says it's about time we found a way to bring more people to Goldstrike."

Another thud from above jiggled the overhead fans. Gaby slapped her charcoal down on the sketch and glared upward.

"Barney said he'll probably be able to add on to Hacienda Heaven in no time once all them tourists start pourin' into town."

Gaby gritted her teeth and met Char's innocently blank eyes.

"Barney said —"

"When are you and Barney going to tie that knot everyone's always talking about?" Gaby asked with false cheeriness.

Shirley pursed her lips. "Maybe never. I've had me two husbands already and neither of 'em brought anything but trouble."

A fresh assault in the upstairs regions made the ceiling tremble. "*Men* never bring anything but trouble, period," Gaby said darkly. "Why don't you cut out, Shirley? It's almost five."

Immediately the plump, blond woman flipped off the steamer. "Don't mind if I do. Promised I'd go give Barney a hand." She quickly tidied the pieces assembled before her and went to gather her bag.

He isn't up there, Gaby thought. *Jacques Ledan isn't the type to involve himself with overseeing the small stuff.* She picked up the stick of charcoal once more. *Don't let me have to look him in the eye again. Why did I let him kiss me?* She hadn't *let* him. He'd . . . well, he'd lulled her into not really noticing what he was doing . . . until he'd . . . Gaby rested her elbows on the bench and covered her face. Heat flooded every part of her, and some of those parts ached in a way she didn't want to examine too closely.

"Bye!" Shirley called.

Gaby glanced up. "Bye. See you tomorrow."

Once the door closed behind Shirley, Gaby ground her fists into her eyes. She just couldn't bear the idea of having to face Jacques Ledan and know he knew what she was thinking — what they would both be thinking.

"Okay. Let's have it."

Startled, Gaby turned to Char. "Have what?"

"The whole story. Yesterday you left Sis's with the bozo and didn't get back for an hour and a half. What happened?"

Gaby gaped.

"He's a knockout, isn't he?" Char's cloud of springy gray curls bobbed with the toss of her head. "Tall, dark, blue-eyed and knock-'em-dead good-looking?"

"When did you see —"

76

"Ah-hah!" Char wagged a long finger. "So the reports are true. Where did he take you and what did the two of you do?"

"I don't *believe* this." Gaby realized she'd crushed the charcoal, and tried to brush oily black dust from her fingers. "Sophie tattled! Not that there's anything to tattle about. I simply wanted to take the opportunity to tell Ledan where we stand in this town."

"For an hour and a half?" Char said, squinting at a row of small pump bottles. "Drove off toward Odles' place, so Caleb at the garage said. In a big Jeep. The one we've seen going through town, only we didn't know it was Ledan's."

"We decided we'd talk better in private," Gaby said lamely.

"*We* decided." Char sprayed a mist from one bottle into the air and sniffed. "Banana. I don't know about this idea of making the fruit smell authentic. You and Ledan already became a *we*. Sounds promising."

"Promising?"

"Do you like him?"

"*No!*"

Char smirked. "Too emphatic, darling. You do like him."

"I *hate* him!"

"Very narrow line between love and hate. Did you wonder what it would be like if he kissed you?"

An immediate flood of heat washed Gaby's face.

"Yippie!" Char twirled, spraying essence of banana as she went. "You didn't just think about it. You *found out!*"

"You don't know —"

"Yes I do. I'm clairvoyant. Good. I'm glad. It's long past time for you to have a man in your life again. Michael Copeland was a dud, but —"

"Michael is Mae's father and he's a good . . . well, an interesting man. He wasn't right for me, but neither was I right for him."

Char hoisted herself to sit on the edge of a bench. "As I was about to say. Just because Michael Copeland's a dud, it doesn't mean every man is. Jacques Ledan will probably do Goldstrike some good. And if he can do you some good at the same time, I'm all for it."

"Char!"

"There's no substitute for good sex, my girl. You've been celibate far too long, and before you know where you are you'll be a dried up old bag like me."

Gaby flapped a hand. "You amaze me. That —" she pointed weakly toward the upper story of the building "— that opportunist is going to turn this lovely place into a zoo, and all you can think about is . . ."

"Go on. What?"

"All you can think about is getting me into bed with him. I don't know what's gotten into you."

"I believe in making the best of things. He plans to build a little hotel and some shops and maybe put up some mining displays. Big deal. We could use something new around here."

"*Little hotel? Shops?* You don't know the half of it. Try a wild teen center in the old school-house. Try a *theme park.* When Jacques Ledan finishes with us we're never going to be the same — ouch!" A blur of white shot from above and something sharp hit Gaby's cheek.

"That came through the skylight," Char said.

"No kidding." Scowling, Gaby picked up a sleek paper airplane. "What a dumb stunt."

Char craned her neck to peer out the skylight. "There's a man up there. He's waving."

"I bet he is," Gaby mumbled, knowing who she would see if she looked.

"Tall, dark, blue-eyed and knock-'em-dead handsome, unless I'm much mistaken," Char reported in rapt tones.

"Yeah."

"Wave to him, Gaby."

Feeling yet another dull flush creep up her neck, Gaby raised her chin. The window where Jacques stood had always been closed. Now it was open, and he leaned his weight on the sill — and smiled that smile she was unlikely ever to forget.

"He's got a mean aim," Char said.

"Yeah. Doesn't he?" Gaby rubbed her cheek. "Some people never grow up."

"He's trying to tell you something."

"I'd like to tell *him* something."

"I bet the plane's a note. Open it up and see."

"No." Gaby threw the plane on the bench and fished a fresh box of charcoal from a drawer.

"Then I will."

Gaby snatched back the plane as Char made a grab. "All right. All right." Even at a distance, Jacques's teeth shone. "Stupidity. Throwing paper planes like a little kid." She unfolded the paper, read, then pressed it to her chest when Char tried to see what he'd written.

"What does it say?"

"Nothing." Gaby made to crumple the paper, caught Char's eye and pushed it into a pocket instead.

"Oh, come on." Char sidled closer. "You can't *do* this to me. What does the note say?"

"Nothing."

"Yes it does."

"No, it doesn't." Why did she wish so badly that whatever game the man was playing wasn't just that — a game?

"I'll go on upstairs and thank him for it anyway and tell him you agree. How's that?"

Char put down the bottle and turned toward the door.

"He wants me to have dinner with him," Gaby said in a rush. "At that wretched La Place. Can you imagine the nerve of the man?"

"He wants you to have dinner?" Char repeated slowly. "Accept."

"I will not." But she wanted to.

"Wave and nod."

"No."

"Then I'll go and tell him for you." Char headed for the door again.

"No! Char, don't you dare do any such thing. He's only trying to get me in his corner because he doesn't want any opposition to his plans."

"I bet he kisses wonderfully."

"What?" Gaby leapt to her feet. "Char, I can't believe you're talking like this."

Char shrugged. "Great aim with a paper plane. Stands to reason a man with that kind of aim would be marvelous at kissing — and other things. He'd be bound to do other things with a lot of flair and authority."

"This is bizarre. You must be tired. Why don't you go home early?"

"You did like the way he kissed you?"

"Yes, but — I never said he kissed me."

Char nodded with apparent satisfaction. She leaned forward to peer at Jacques. "Gone," she said, sounding disappointed.

"Use your head, girl. Even if you don't want to have an affair with him, it won't hurt to get close enough to be on the inside of whatever his plans are."

"You are definitely not yourself," Gaby said. "There's no reason I can't go home and sketch. You stay here and fantasize. I'll go to my place and work. Michael's expecting the drawings for *Dogs* by next week."

"And since Michael's always been so trustworthy and timely himself, we wouldn't want to keep him waiting, would we?"

Gaby picked up a natural straw hat with a wide brim that turned up and crammed it low over her brows. "Michael did get me the work for the film," she reminded Char.

"Because you're the best there is at what you do," Char said tartly. "Go on home. But make sure you give some thought to tall, dark and —"

"Knock-'em-dead handsome," Gaby concluded for her. "Not if I can help it." But she probably wouldn't have any choice.

Letting herself out by the back entrance, Gaby walked into the courtyard where she kept her bike . . . and stopped.

Littered all over the red tiles and caught in the fronds of purple bougainvillea that trailed from painted planters atop a white stucco wall, were pieces of white paper — pieces of white paper folded into sleek airplanes.

Gaby shook her head, picked one up and

unfolded: "Have dinner with me tonight. It's time you saw La Place from the inside. Jacques."

She retrieved another and another and opened each one: "Have dinner with me tonight . . ."

A slow smile formed on Gaby's mouth. She pulled her battered bicycle upright before turning back to look again at the upstairs window. Once more he watched her and this time she did wave — and let the papers flutter, one by one, from her fingers. The thought of him trying, again and again, to get one of his silly concoctions through her skylight brought immense satisfaction. It shouldn't please her so much that he'd been determined to capture her attention, but it did.

Great aim Jacques Ledan didn't have. Great kissing technique, he did. The jury was still out on the rest of his skills. But the jury hadn't adjourned — not yet.

5

He almost fell down the stairs.

Scrambling to catch his balance, Jacques skidded through the hallway and burst into the street. Without pausing, he gained the Jeep, vaulted into the driver's seat and gunned the engine to life. In seconds he shot around a corner and instantly brought his quarry into sight. His *prey*, as Bart called Gaby.

She rode at a leisurely pace, arms braced straight against the handlebars of the decrepit bike. The brim of the straw hat flapped, and her hair and skirts floated behind.

Jacques steered the Jeep's nose beside Gaby's back wheel and crawled. When the bike wobbled dangerously, he grinned and rested an elbow on top of his door. "Nice afternoon!"

She wobbled even more, then gained control and kept right on riding — and ignoring him.

"Didn't your mother tell you it's dangerous to ride a bike in a skirt?"

"Why?"

"It might get caught in the wheel and yank you off." He edged forward until he was beside her. "Or maybe just yank your skirt off. That would probably embarrass you."

"I don't embarrass easily."

He grinned. "Good."

Gaby looked at him sharply and there was no mistaking the tinge of red in her cheeks.

Jacques was suddenly aware of how good he felt. "So — what do you say?"

She frowned at him. "About what?"

"Will you?"

"Will I?" She backpedaled to a halt. "Will I *what?*"

Jacques braked and backed up. "Let me entertain you? At La Place? For dinner . . . or whatever?"

Gaby planted her feet on the dusty pavement. "You haven't invited me."

"Yes I have." He tipped his face up to a sky as crystal-bright blue as only a California sky could be. "I invited you over and over again. It wasn't easy getting one of those invitations through that skylight."

"And into my face."

He looked at her. "It didn't hit you?"

"It certainly did." Holding the crown of the hat, she tilted her cheek. "See?"

Swiftly Jacques killed the engine and got out of the Jeep. "Let me see that." Before she could react, he held her face in his hands and used a thumb to prop her chin. "Well, hell, I'm mighty sorry about that, ma'am."

"It's all right." She closed a hand over his wrist and pulled. "Think nothing of it."

Jacques made no attempt to release her. "Afraid that's not possible, ma'am. I'll have to make amends." With that, he kissed her soft skin very gently. "Mmm. Reckon that ought to make it all better."

He felt her tremble and lean — ever so slightly — toward him. Dropping his hands to her shoulders, Jacques looked down into brilliant green eyes that seemed vaguely out of focus. Her lips parted and she held the tip of her tongue in her teeth.

"Is it better?" he breathed, expanding his lungs and flexing his thighs against an aching jolt.

Gaby's eyes slowly regained focus and grew sharper. "Oh, I don't get this." Pushing away his hands, she mounted the bicycle. "I don't *do* this kind of thing. I'm a mature, sensible woman who — I just don't get it." Muttering, she bent over the handlebars and stood on the pedals of the gearless machine to pump furiously.

"I get it," Jacques said to himself. "I know exactly what this is all about." He would let her get ahead — maybe even allow her to think he'd given up and skulked away. He already knew where she lived.

The small, picture-book-pretty, white stucco house that Gaby called home wasn't more than a ten-minute drive from the hat factory. Jacques waited until she was out of sight before inching the Jeep to the next corner and waiting again.

Gaby took not ten, but twenty, minutes — pedaling rapidly — to reach her home. No doubt the bike was an occasional nod to fitness . . . not that he'd seen anything to suggest she wasn't in great shape. Jacques grinned broadly. Yeah, the lady was in great shape.

"Hey, Gaby!" Swerving into the pink gravel driveway, he hailed her as she opened her front door. "We've got things to discuss."

Gaby walked into the house and shut the door.

Jacques switched off the ignition and got out. Something was happening to him, something different. And he liked it. He leaned against the Jeep, tossed his keys in the air and caught them. There were a host of acquaintances who wouldn't believe this scene. Jacques Ledan supposedly always waited for people to come to him. Jacques didn't chase, hadn't chased, until Gaby McGregor.

He shrugged away from the Jeep, jammed his hands into his pockets and sauntered toward the house. Not a chase . . . a hunt. There was a subtle difference. And, possibly without knowing, Gaby was adding to the fascination. *Country bumpkin . . . hayseed.* Remembering Bart's sneering comments,

Jacques narrowed his eyes. Without being sure why, he was convinced there was more to Gaby than the obvious — much more.

Oleander, pink, white and peach colored, still bloomed in plantings near the house. Jade bushes glistened in groups of terra cotta pots. Jacques reached the door and knocked.

From inside came the muted tones of a male ballad singer.

Jacques rested a shoulder on the jamb and waited. He knew with some deep part of him that they were both playing a game. She didn't want him to give up, any more than he intended to do so.

Across the wide, potholed street, fence posts, linked together by sagging wires, sloped at drunken angles. Yellow brush bent in the warm, dust-laden breeze of a late-October afternoon, and on the horizon sunlight danced and glittered, turning yellow to gold. This was his country and it made him feel alive.

He raised a hand, bowed his head and knocked again, much louder this time.

Rapid footsteps approached. The door opened wide. "Are you bored, or what?" She crossed her arms — a pleasing sight given what happened to the thin, white cotton shirt.

"I've never been less bored." Amazingly it was true.

"You must lead a really quiet life."

"May I come in?"

"No."

"Just for a little while? To talk?"

Gaby raised a hand to smooth escaped pieces of hair. "Absolutely not."

Jacques didn't even try not to look at the way her breasts — she wasn't wearing a bra — moved when she angled up her elbow. "We need to talk. We've got things to discuss."

"We've got nothing to discuss."

"Do you believe in . . . Do you think that sometimes two people are wildly attracted on sight?"

"I think most men are attracted to anything in a skirt on sight."

He let out an explosive laugh. "You aren't subtle, Gaby."

"I'm honest." She stood aside. "All right. Come in and have something to drink. But I'm not going to play games with you, Jacques. Becoming a diversion to a bored city type isn't my idea of a good time."

"We ought to talk about what each of us considers a good time." He paused in the act of passing her and looked down. "You have a wonderful face. Do lots of men tell you that?"

"Dozens every day." A small smile tipped up the corners of her generous mouth. "I have to fight them off."

"I know what you mean. So do I — fight off the women."

"I believe you," she said and the smile left her face. "Which makes me very puzzled about you, Jacques Ledan. Why are you following me around?"

She was tiny of stature, small-boned with slender arms and ankles — ankles were all he'd seen of her legs to date beneath the long skirts she favored. A belt, made of bold silver links, loosely circled her small waist.

"You know why I'm following you," he said, entering a cool, white-walled foyer with woven hala rugs atop a terrazzo floor. "I can't help myself and I don't want to."

"Tea, coffee, soda, wine or beer?" She led the way down a hallway to an airy kitchen, white again but made striking by dark green accents. "I'm having a white wine cooler."

"So am I."

"What is it you think we have to discuss?"

"Our future." Instinct told him he'd have to corner her or fail — he didn't do failure at all well.

"You think you're amusing, don't you?" Ice clinked into glasses and Gaby splashed in wine and soda. "For some reason you've decided I'd make an entertaining mouse to your cat."

Did she really think that? "Wrong. We didn't get off to a great start. I'm sorry for that."

"We didn't get off to a start at all. Here."

He took the glass she handed him and

tipped it back and forth. "What would you call what happened between us yesterday?"

"A mistake."

The tightness in her voice meant he didn't have to look at her to know she was blushing. "You embarrass easily, don't you?"

"I told you I don't get embarrassed."

"Yes you do." He drank deeply. "I kissed you and you liked it. You liked it a lot."

"Have you finished your drink?"

Now he did look at her. Those green eyes, the instant before she looked away, were brilliant and deeply troubled. "I haven't finished my drink, Gaby. I haven't finished anything as far as you're concerned. Would you believe me if I said I was as caught off guard by what happened between us as you were?"

She spread her fingers on the pale skin at the neck of her shirt. "I don't know you well enough to believe or disbelieve anything you say. It's getting late and —"

"I've got all the time in the world. My plans for Goldstrike are a different issue from what's happening between you and me —"

"*Nothing's* happening."

A minor topic switch might lull her into relaxing. "Cycling is good exercise."

Gaby frowned and shook her head.

"It must be nice not to have to drive your car to work every day."

"I don't have a car." There was almost a defiance in the way she told him.

"Isn't that inconvenient sometimes? I mean, you must have to transport things occasionally."

"Goldstrike's a generous place. Everyone knows I don't have a car anymore. If I need help, I get it. That must seem odd to a man like you." She swirled the drink in her glass.

Jacques considered. "Like me? I thought you'd decided you don't know me."

"I don't."

This wasn't improving. He made himself smile. "You will." And maybe he'd wise up. She probably couldn't afford a car. A single woman running a hat factory in a hick town was likely to live hand to mouth. "Were you ever married?" *Oh, very smooth.*

"Yes."

"Is there anyone else now?" He wouldn't blame her for refusing to answer.

Gaby showed no sign of offense. "There's no one else."

So, there was no impediment there. He was free to pursue. "I used to like riding a bike."

Gaby stared, then puffed up her cheeks. "The topic changes from marriage to bikes. Okay. When was that — when you rode bikes, I mean? Before you became a candy king?"

"I'm not . . ." *No.* She had no way of knowing how sick he was that for most people he was a product rather than a man. "Yeah. Before I became a candy king. Just call me luscious Ledan and I'll know you're not talking to anyone but me."

Regarding him speculatively, she sipped her drink. "What's it like to be filthy, stinking rich?"

That was a novel approach. "Past a certain point, money doesn't have much actual meaning."

"You haven't answered my question."

"I think I have."

"Mmm." She rolled her frosty wineglass against her jaw. "So, you're so used to being wealthy it doesn't mean anything anymore. And you think having the corner on chocolate-covered truffles gives you the right to have whatever you want — even if you only want it for a short while and even if you might do damage by having it at all."

Jacques narrowed his eyes. "What are we talking about here?"

Gaby lowered her gaze. "Nothing, I guess. I was just thinking aloud and not making much sense."

Sure. Only he didn't believe her. And neither was he confused about her meaning. "I don't ever set out to hurt people, Gaby." The local populace wasn't the issue here. She assumed he used women as diversions and that he intended her to become his temporary antiboredom device. "We interest each other."

"Do we?" Almost absently, she set her glass

on a tiled counter and turned to look through the window at well-tended plantings in a courtyard enclosed by a white stone wall.

Jacques went to stand behind her. "We're very attracted to each other." Her hat had been discarded. A hint of red gleamed in her black hair. "We are, Gaby. Admit it."

She glanced back at him. "The kind of attraction you're talking about can be dangerous to the health."

"Sometimes." He smoothed her hair carefully, from the crown of her head, to within inches of her waist. "But you aren't denying you feel it."

"No."

At this first hint of victory his muscles tensed. "Good." Cautious not to make any sudden moves, Jacques slipped his hand beneath her hair to settle loosely on her nape. "This kind of attraction doesn't happen often, Gaby. We've got to make the best of it." He rubbed his thumb up and down the side of her neck.

Gaby sighed and smiled up at him. "This is some line."

"You and I are two magnets on a collision course. We — What did you say?"

"I said, this is some line. You must have had a lot of practice."

He smothered a laugh. "This is no line, sweetheart." This lady would never be dull. "I know what I feel and you feel it, too.

We're going to have to do something about it."

"You're a dreamer."

"I certainly am." Jacques closed his eyes. "You should see what I'm dreaming. We're just going to have to make my dreams come true . . . and yours."

"I'm not dreaming. My eyes are wide open."

She was going to make this very difficult. Jacques didn't entirely dislike that idea. "Don't tell me you haven't thought, at least briefly, about how we would be together."

"No! . . . Yes." The last was said as if it cost her dearly.

Jacques grinned and turned her toward him. "Good. Now we've settled the preliminary stuff. Why don't we go up to my place?"

"Go up to your place?"

"We could have a nice, intimate little dinner. Swim some, maybe . . . or maybe not." What did he see in her eyes? "If you'd rather, we'll just light a fire, and . . ."

"And?"

Her face was turned up to his. Jacques looked at her moist, slightly parted lips and almost forgot her question. "And we could get to know each other better." Slowly he brought his mouth closer to Gaby's.

"Better than what?" She settled her hands on his chest.

The shadow between her breasts showed at

the open neck of her shirt. A breath raised that full, soft flesh. Jacques felt his body harden. Her nipples stiffened against the thin, white cotton.

Jacques brought his lips even nearer to Gaby's. "Better and better. Just better and better." He cupped her breasts, closed his eyes and drew her bottom lip gently between his teeth. "So much better." His thumbs found the rigid centers of her nipples. He stroked back and forth until she gasped, and then he trapped her hips between the counter and the part of him that was too hard and heavy to ignore.

"Gaby, maybe we should just stay here." One empty house was as good as another if the company was perfect.

"Maybe —" she tried to turn her head aside "— maybe *we* shouldn't stay anywhere."

The uncertainty in her voice brought him satisfaction. "I don't think you mean that."

"There are one or two things . . . one thing you don't know about me."

"Only one?" he murmured. If she thought he hadn't guessed that she was one passionate woman, she was wrong. "Kiss me, Gaby."

The sound of the front door slamming reverberated through the house. "Didn't you close that?" He brushed the backs of his fingers across her cheek.

"Yes." Before he could react, she ducked from his grasp.

Footsteps clattered in the hall leading to the kitchen. "Mom! Where are you?"

"In here," Gaby called.

6

"Mom, there's a truck out front." The small girl who burst into the room needed little introduction. Jacques wiped any sign of surprise from his face and put on his best benevolent expression for Gaby McGregor's daughter.

"Jacques," Gaby said, glowing with obvious parental pride. "This is Mae."

He put his hands in his pockets. "Hi, Mae. How are you?" So much for his assumptions about lack of impediments and empty houses.

The child accepted a hug from Gaby without taking her dark brown eyes from Jacques's face. Once released, she wrinkled her nose and asked, "Who's he?"

"Mae! Don't be rude." Gaby planted her hands on her hips, but chuckled fondly. "This is Mr. Ledan. The truck is a Jeep. It belongs to him."

"I remember *him!* He's the one who sat at The Table at Sis's."

"Your mother and I are friends." He deliberately relaxed his clenched jaw. "You can call me Jacques, if you like."

"Mommy doesn't like me to call people by their first names if we don't know them."

Jacques looked at Gaby. "I just told you your mother and I are friends." Gaby bit her lip and didn't quite suppress a smile. She was enjoying his discomfort, damn it.

Mae braced her thin legs apart and accomplished a ferocious frown. "Is he from Los Angles, like Daddy?"

"Um —"

"Yes." Jacques cut Gaby off. "At least, I have a house in Los Angeles. But I've got one here, too."

"No, you don't."

Enough of the kindness-to-little-children bit. Jacques frowned right back. "Yes I do."

"No you don't." Mae McGregor approached, her familiarly sharp little chin thrust forward. "If you lived in Goldstrike I'd know where your house is. I don't. So you don't."

Gaby cleared her throat. "Mae —"

"Have you ever seen the house just outside town? The one all on its own up in the foothills?"

For an instant Mae's frown grew even darker. Then her finely drawn eyebrows rose. "The os-osterentious monster . . . monsterous . . . Does he mean that one, Mommy? The osterentious —"

"Mae, hush," Gaby said.

Jacques gave her a wicked grin. "That's the one, Mae. Ostentatious monstrosity? Is that what your mother calls it?"

"Uh-huh. A lot of people do." She shook her head, whipping a shiny black ponytail back and forth. "I've never seen it. I know it's big, though. Too big to be useful — that's what Mommy said. But that's probably because you aren't from around here, so you don't know what your house is supposed to be like. Sophie always says it's nice to try to make excuses for other people when they do dumb stuff."

This time Jacques didn't trust himself to meet Gaby's eyes. "That's very generous of Sophie. And very nice of you, too. But I do come from around here, really. My grand-father built La — he built the house you're talking about. That was just before I was born and I've been spending time there since I was a boy."

"Jeez." Mae's frown slid back into place. "It's a real old house, then. I 'spect it's a whole lot older than ours, huh?"

"I wouldn't be surprised." He'd never had much to do with children. Until today his excuse would have been lack of oppor-tunity — after this encounter the explana-tion was likely to be markedly different.

"How was school, Mae?" Gaby sounded strangled.

"Same as always. Do you have any animals at that house?"

100

"Mae, it isn't polite to —"

"Yes," Jacques said.

Mae sighed hugely inside a sleeveless, red and white cotton dress. "*Everybody* does," she said with a dramatic flap of spindly arms. "Everybody but me."

"You like animals?" He saw the possibility of a crack in the child's apparent dislike of him. There was nothing like empathy to win over a female.

"I *love* animals." The scowl was redirected at Gaby. "Mom won't let me have any."

"Mae, this isn't the time or place to discuss —"

"When I was a boy I had all kinds of animals. What's your favorite?"

Mae clasped her hands and considered. "I love dogs."

"You're allergic to them," Gaby said in a voice that should have warned Mae to tread carefully.

"I love cats, too."

"You're allergic to cats. That's why we don't have dogs or cats. That and the fact that I don't think people should have animals if they aren't around to look after them."

"Cats can be left alone," Jacques told her, smiling benignly.

"It doesn't matter. Mae's —"

"Allergic to them," Jacques finished for her. "So you've said." He made sure his eyes said what he couldn't say aloud, that she should have told him she had a child. His next thought was about the father of that child. It came as an unpleasant surprise to discover he could dislike someone he'd never met.

"Many people are allergic to dander," Gaby said. "Mae, Jacques makes candy."

"He does?" Interest flickered in the girl's eyes. "I never knew men made candy. My grandma lives in Portland — the one in Oregon — and she makes fudge and salt-water taffy and sends it sometimes. When we visited one time she let me help. The kitchen got real hot. I like helping in kitchens. Could I come to your house and help?"

"Mr. Ledan doesn't exactly —"

"Sure you can come. I'll be sure we get to make some really unusual stuff." One of the positives about children was that they were generally uncomplicated — they could be bought.

"Mr. Ledan doesn't actually *make* the candy himself," Gaby said. Her face no longer betrayed anything of what she was thinking. "He owns big factories that mass-produce the stuff."

"Stuff?" Jacques pretended affront. "Factories? Ledan's candies are made in kitchens, madam. And they are referred to as confectionery, not *stuff*. I'll arrange a special demonstration for you, Mae — in the kitchen at my house. Would you like that?"

"Boy, yes. Wait till I tell the other kids."

"You'll get to visit my dog, too." He saw Gaby prepare to protest and held up both hands. "Spike's not really long-haired and I'll make sure —"

"No dog is short-haired enough," Gaby said and added, grudgingly, "but thank you, anyway."

"I told Mary-Alice Healy I'm getting a pig."

"You're not supposed to talk to Mary-Alice Healy. The last time you did the pair of you got into trouble for pulling hair and — What did you say?"

"I told her I'm getting a pig," Mae told her mother in a very small voice.

Jacques hid a grin.

"Mae! Why did you tell a fib like that?"

The girl displayed Gaby's talent for brilliant blushes. "I said it 'cause she's always braggin'. *She's* got a dog *and* a cat and her dad says she can have a pony when she's ten. So I said I'm gonna get a pig for my seven and a half birthday."

"When's that?" Jacques asked innocently.

"In a week."

"Well, young lady," Gaby said. "We don't celebrate half-year birthdays around here. And you're just going to have to admit that you fibbed."

Mae shook her head violently and pressed her lips together.

"This is all I needed," Gaby muttered,

and Jacques observed her speculatively. "We'll talk about the consequences of lying later, Mae."

"Daddy would buy me a pig."

"Mae," Gaby said warningly.

"Who do you look like most?" Jacques asked Mae. "Your mom or your dad?"

Mae glowered at Gaby. "My *dad*. He's a lot of fun, too." She gave Jacques her full attention. "If you and Mom are friends, why haven't I seen you before?"

"We only met a little while ago." Sometimes honesty was the best route.

"So why are you here today?"

"I came to invite your mother to dinner. I'm waiting for her to tell me she'll come."

"Oh." Mae pursed her lips. "When Daddy comes he eats here with Mommy and me."

"Ah-hah." Evidently he'd made an even bigger error than he'd thought in assessing the situation.

"My dad's tall. Much taller than you."

"Really?" He looked at Gaby over Mae's head. Gaby rolled her eyes. "I guess your daddy's much younger and better looking, too."

Mae nodded. "Much. Char says he's the best looking man she ever saw. Char works for Mom. Mom thinks so, too, don't you, Mom?"

Gaby made a noise that sounded vaguely like an agreement.

104

"And Daddy's an artist. You aren't, are you?"

"No."

"Daddy's very clever. He's made all kinds of money and he likes giving me things . . . and Mom."

The kid was challenging him. "I bet he loves you a great deal and that's why he likes giving you things." *Everything but himself.* Jacques felt in his pocket for his keys. "Does your daddy get up here to see you often?"

"All the time." She puffed up her cheeks and expelled the air upward at wisps of hair. "He'll be coming to stay with us again soon, won't he, Mommy?"

Jacques caught the faint shake of Gaby's head — and the worried shadow in her eyes, but she said, "I expect so. We mustn't keep Jacques any longer."

He pulled out the keys and managed a smile. "I'll call you tomorrow about that dinner date." Gaby wasn't the type to lie easily, and she'd said she was single. So the daughter was a complication, but all bets were still on.

"We've got all kinds of stuff to do, don't we, Mom?" Mae leaned on the table. "Mom doesn't go out on dates. That's what you're talking about, isn't it? Taking Mom out on a date?"

"I guess it is," he said, watching the child's edgy wiggling back and forth. "Would that be okay?" It was natural that she felt threatened — particularly if Gaby hadn't seen many men since she was divorced. He assumed she was divorced.

Mae ignored him. She knelt on a chair and rested her chin on a fist.

Jacques touched Gaby's shoulder, stroked to her elbow and back. "Don't bother to come with me. I can see myself out." She looked, not at him but at Mae. "Call you tomorrow," he told her.

"Yes," Gaby agreed distractedly. "Thank you."

In the hall Jacques deliberately pulled the kitchen door shut behind him.

Before the latch clicked he heard Mae say, "He's not bad, Mom, but Daddy's nicer."

Gaby responded, "You don't know Jacques yet."

He took his hand from the doorknob and sauntered from the house. Once in the Jeep, with his arms spread along the back of the seat, he slid down to rest his head back and squint at the sparkling, late-afternoon sky.

You don't know Jacques yet.

In a quiet way, the lady had defended him. "Oh, yeah," he whispered to the warm air. "Oh, *yeah!*" The day hadn't turned out exactly as expected, but progress had definitely been made.

7

"We've got to stay calm and clearheaded," Sophie announced. "And we've got to be smarter and more organized than he is."

Gaby accepted the mug of coffee Sis offered and listened to murmurs of assent from Caleb. "Change the place, he would," he muttered. "Wouldn't be the same. O'course, it'd be good for business. All those tourists would be bound to buy a heap o' gas, and —" he caught Sophie's narrowed gaze "— and, well, wouldn't be worth it, no how."

"How come he's suddenly visible all over the place, that's what I'd like to know," Sophie said. "According to the talk that's going around he's been visiting that monstrosity of a house since he was a boy. Don't believe it, myself. If he had been, we'd all know him by now."

"I believe it," Gaby said and quickly tipped her mug.

"How would you know?" This time it was Char who spoke from a chair pulled up to the end of the booth where Gaby sat with

Sophie Byler, Caleb and Shirley. Sis hovered nearby.

"I've spoken to someone who knows all about him," Gaby said evasively. "Don't ask me to tell you who because I can't break a confidence." It wasn't exactly a lie.

"Barney says he thinks we should go along with Ledan's plans," Shirley commented. "He says this town's going to die, anyways, the way things are going, so why not grab a chance to make some money."

Sophie leaned over the table. "And what do *you* say about that, Shirley?"

"Well, I could use more money as much as anyone, but I was born and bred in Goldstrike and I don't want it turned into no — what did you call it, Gaby?"

"Plastic playground." Jacques's eyes were the kind of dark blue that burned. When he'd looked at her on Monday, just before he'd kissed — started kissing her — they'd turned almost black. And when he smiled they warmed, but in a way that made her want him to heat her from skin to bone and everywhere in between. She pressed her stomach, but it wasn't her stomach that ached. "He —"

"Gaby?"

She started. "Yes?"

Sophie's pale blue eyes speared her. "What's the matter with you? This is important and you're daydreaming."

"Sorry," Gaby said sheepishly, not missing Char's raised brows. "I was thinking about things, that's all." On Tuesday and again on Wednesday, Jacques had stood at the window above the workroom until Gaby obligingly saw him — and immediately turned away. Yesterday she'd returned his wave. This meeting had been called for eight in the morning, and Gaby had yet to go to the workroom. Would he be at the window again? A small stab of apprehension turned her stomach.

"We're going to circulate petitions."

"How could you be so *dumb*," Gaby muttered. He was playing some game, and if she chose to play, too, she'd undoubtedly end up the loser.

"Dumb?" Sophie folded her fingers around Gaby's forearm.

Gaby jumped again. "No, no, I was talking to myself. I've got a lot on my mind, what with the movie work to do and now this nuisance with Jacques."

"So, he's Jacques now," Char remarked, nonchalantly consulting her date book. "I'm glad you're on good terms with him. That could be very useful."

"I'm *not* on any kind of terms with him." Now *that* was a lie. "And if I were I wouldn't use that type of situation against him."

"There cannot be a theme park in this

town," Sophie said with finality. "It would ruin —"

"Hush," Sis said, surprising everyone at the table. She clamped her lips together and jerked her head toward the door.

Gaby craned around and saw Bart Stanly coming in with a sleekly elegant blond woman. They made a move toward The Table.

"S'taken!" Sis hollered, loudly enough to make everyone in the place jump.

Bart, healthily handsome and solid in an olive-green suit and tan shirt, glanced around with apparently guileless confusion. "I don't see anyone waiting." He plopped one of the tipped chairs down and stood back for his companion to sit. "You're going to love this place, Camilla. It's so hokey it's unreal."

Gaby cringed and saw her companions wince in unison.

"Chairs is tipped," Sis announced. "Chairs is tipped for my kin on account of they're comin' for breakfast. They wouldn't be none too pleased if I was to let you used their tipped chairs and their table, so I reckon as you'd better take a booth . . . less'n you'd as well go somewheres else."

"Did you hear that?" Caleb whispered loudly. "I never heard that female say more'n two words at a stretch before. Now she's spoutin' as bad as my old lady."

"If'n you'd like a change from this here

110

hokey place, you'd probably do real fine over at Barney's place." Sis's voice sounded rusty, like the coughing motor of a hand-cranked vintage car. "Down the road a spell. Hacienda Heaven it's called these days. Used to be a plain old tavern afore Barney visited that Teejuana. That's a foreign place. Mexico. Don't hold with travelin' meself. Gives a body ideas that don't do a bit o' good."

Gaby put a hand over her mouth to smother a giggle.

"Whoa," Char said in a low voice. "She's really on a roll. May never stop."

"Barney makes what he calls burners. On account of they're hot, I guess. Nasty things in tough fried stuff he twists up in half. Anything he's got. That's what he puts in 'em. That and a heap of that hot sauce."

Seconds of silence followed, and Gaby didn't trust herself to look at Sis, or her victims.

"Thank you for the recommendation," Bart finally said. "But we'll use a booth. Some of your lovely hot coffee would be a wonderful start. And I'd like a stack of those spectacular blueberry pancakes you make. With the boysenberry syrup. How about you, Camilla?"

"Would you listen to him sucking up to Sis?" Caleb hissed.

"Won't do him any good," Shirley said matter-of-factly.

The door opened again and Caleb's skinny wife, Esther, rushed in. As usual, her florid face glowed. "Darn, but I thought I'd never get over here. Got stuck on the phone, but at least it was about the petition. We aren't going to have to twist arms to get support on this one. I doubt there's a body in this town who wants anything to do with no theme park." If Esther noticed the frantic gesturing from those seated, she showed no sign.

"I don't reckon there's too many thrilled about the durn youth center, neither," she continued. "We'd better get those petitions printed up and fast. I hear Ledan's already got himself a whole office suite being finished for him above Gaby's place. Cal said as how there's not no expense being spared. And some lackey of Ledan's was tellin' him about an expert who'd be arrivin' in a few days. An expert in *theme* parks, if you can imagine such a fool thing. We'd better organize getting the signatures right now."

Gaby pretended great interest in her coffee.

Caleb began whistling an off-key rendition of "At the End of the Rainbow" and Gaby kicked him under the table.

"Whatcha do that for?"

"Shut up, Caleb," Char glared at him.

"And you, Esther, keep your voice down."

Gaby felt Bart approach but didn't look up. "Good morning, all," he said too pleasantly. "How are we today?"

"I'm fine," Shirley said. "Can't speak for you or anyone else."

"I'm fine, too, Bart," Gaby said with a smile.

"Good, good." He waved a hand expansively in his companion's direction. "This is Camilla Roberts — an old friend of mine, but mostly of Jacques's. She happened to be passing through the area and decided to drop in for a visit."

Char leaned close to Gaby. "Passing through?" she mumbled. "Nobody *passes through* Goldstrike."

Bart bowed his head toward Char. "I beg your pardon?"

"I said lucky day for Goldstrike." She smiled up at him.

Camilla Roberts rose from her seat and came to Bart's side. Promptly he put an arm around her shoulders. "Camilla and Jacques have known each other for years," he said as if he were talking to Jacques Ledan's personal cheering squad.

"That's right," Camilla said in a husky voice guaranteed to melt any man's socks — and strategic points north of his feet. She flipped back the silky curve of her long, honey-colored hair. "I can hardly wait to see

113

him again. Don't you think this idea of his for your little town is just *wonderful?*"

No one responded.

Gaby's eyes flicked to Bart's face, and she saw his mouth tighten. Mr. Stanly was no fool and he'd overheard the conversation about petitions to oust Jacques and his *wonderful* ideas.

"I'm a beauty consultant," Camilla continued, widening large and admittedly beautiful brown eyes. She gave Bart a playful poke with a long, pale pink fingernail. "And Bart forgot to let me know the spa is already past the blueprint stage."

"Spa?" Sophie and Gaby spoke in unison. "What spa?"

Camilla smoothed skin-tight black suede pants over her hips and pulled up the collar on her black silk blouse. "Don't pretend I'm not the last to learn that Jacques's spa plans are going ahead. I know he intended to offer me the managerial position, because —" she leaned down, showing a considerable amount of cleavage at the neck of the blouse "— because I'm the best and Jacques only hires the best. He's a very discerning man, which is what I like best about him."

Best? Gaby breathed hard through her nose. And just what else did Camilla Roberts like about Jacques?

"A spa." Sophie looked meaningfully around. "Mr. Ledan is planning a spa, folks.

114

What do we think of that?"

"Overwhelming, isn't it," Camilla purred. "Jacques is almost a visionary sometimes. Of course, the candy business is so successful it runs itself, so he needs other outlets for his talents."

The woman's eyes glowed at the very mention of Jacques Ledan's name. Gaby balled her fists in her lap. Twice he'd come on to her as if she were the only woman in the world. Evidently he'd been bored and filling up a little empty time until Camilla "passed through." Hell, but she hated herself for responding to him.

"Why don't I go on over to the print shop for you, Sophie?" Gaby ignored Char's restraining hand and stood up. She nodded at Camilla. "I hope you enjoy your stay. How long did you say you intended to be here, by the way?"

Camilla shrugged and her pouting lips pushed even farther forward. "That depends entirely on Jacques. Whatever he wants, he gets. But I expect most of you already know that." She giggled. "I may be around for a long time and I won't mind a bit."

Gaby picked up her Mary Poppins-style, black felt — complete with cherries bobbing from the brim — and jammed it over her French-braided chignon. Parting her lips in a parody of a smile, she directed herself to Sophie. "I'm going to put every ounce of energy I've got into this," she said, squaring her shoulders. "If I have my way, there'll be no theme park, no hotel, no multiplex cinema, no wretched mining displays with *leprechauns*, for crying out loud. And no *spa!* Starting this morning I'll be campaigning to boot out Jacques Ledan and his crazy schemes."

"Hey!" Bart reached for her arm. "You're a smart woman. You know this is going to be good for everyone. Wait till you start turning out those baseball —"

"Over my dead body." Gaby sidestepped him and headed for the door. "You can tell Jacques-the-wonder-boy that I'm declaring war."

8

Jacques checked his Rolex and leaned on the sill at the open window above Gaby's factory. "She's late."

"Who's late?"

He turned on Rita. "Don't play dumb with me. Not at this hour of the morning and not when I'm uptight."

"How come you're uptight?"

"Damn it, Rita! Cut the smart talk. I'm not in the mood."

Rita crossed one long leg over the other and jiggled the high green pump that dangled from her toes. "I'm trying to inject a little sanity into all this, Jacques. You can't tell me you aren't suffering from some form of wilderness disease. That's all this business with the little hat person is — a reaction to boredom. What you need is a fast trip to LA — and maybe Paris, too."

She stretched a hand toward the phone on the desk that had been moved into the as-yet-unfinished suite. "I'm going to call a few people and see what they've got on for the weekend. I'll arrange for the chopper to pick you up."

Jacques clamped his fingers over hers and set her hand back in her lap. "You don't get it, do you? I'm fed up to the teeth with LA and Paris and parties and smarmy, grinning faces and Yes, sir. No, sir. Whatever you say, sir. That woman —" he pointed downward "— is *real*. I want some of that, Rita — someone real for a change."

"Aha!" She waggled a long finger at him. "A change. Okay. That I can buy. You want a change, an entertaining little oddity to titillate you for a while. And why not? But don't mix up sexual deprivation with something meaningful, for God's sake."

Talking to Rita about anything deeper than a sidewalk puddle was a waste of time. Jacques went back to his study of the view through Gaby's skylight.

"Don't sulk," Rita said, sounding pinched. "It doesn't suit you. Have you looked over the data that came in from the Paris office? Bayard already called this morning. He wants to know what you think."

"I think we're going to make a killing in the Eastern Block." And he should be more excited. He *was* excited at some level, but somehow the thought of even more Ledan shops selling even more Ledan candies didn't have the power to really *thrill* him.

"And?" Rita prompted.

Jacques turned and sat on the window sill.

"And I'm in total agreement with everything Bayard suggests. The man's a genius. Why wouldn't I agree with him?"

"Good!" Straightening her cream linen skirt, Rita got up. She went to a stack of shiny black crates embossed with the gold company logo and opened the top one. "These arrived late yesterday. Bayard sent them with his compliments. I think he's trying to make sure you don't get so tied up with the Goldstrike extravaganza that you lose interest in the main agenda."

"Until we're up and running here, *this* is my main agenda." *Goldstrike and Gaby McGregor.* "What's in the box mountain?"

"Ta-da!" With a flourish, Rita whirled around — a risky feat on four-inch heels — and held aloft a sparkling heap of gold-wrapped bundles. "Isn't Bayard inspired?"

Jacques got up and stuck out a hand. "Gimme."

She dropped the bundles into his fingers. "Pots of gold! Jacques, you've got to call him and tell him this is going to be pure magic."

He eyed the candies doubtfully. "What exactly are we supposed to do with them?"

"Give them away, of course. As . . . well, as kind of party favors, I guess."

"Party favors?" Increasingly there seemed to be times when his employees' declared strokes of brilliance went right over his head.

Rita pulled more candies from the crate

and began heaping them on the desk. "We'll find some locals to dress up as leprechauns and go around handing these out. They can say something like, ooh —" she screwed up her face "— like, welcome to our end of the rainbow. Accept this pot of gold with Jacques Ledan's gratitude . . . and the gratitude of his entire team who hope you'll be as excited about going for the gold in . . . You don't like it, do you?"

"No."

"Do better."

"I will." He plopped a candy bundle in her hand and said, "Welcome to Goldstrike."

Rita's mouth turned down and she pushed back her mass of auburn hair. "Of course, you're right. Simple is best. It's this town, Jacques. I'm going nuts here."

"Why? It's a great place. It'll do you good to live a simple life for a while. Isn't the trailer okay?" He'd had a fleet of luxury trailers moved in ready for the crews who would be part of the planning stages.

"Fine," Rita said without enthusiasm.

"Good." He didn't want to deal with his employees' temperaments right now. Once more he looked through the window. Still there was no sign of life in the workroom. "You'll settle down eventually. I think I'll see if I can finally get Gaby to La Place for dinner tonight."

"You're kidding."

He looked at her sharply. "Why would I be?"

"She's *so* unsophisticated, Jacques. A little nobody who makes caps for the feed store people, or something. Or those cheap straw efforts the men wear in the fields around here. Have some fun, if you want to. Take her to Hacienda Heaven for one of those horrible burner things and . . . well, and whatever else you've got in mind. I hardly think she's the type you invite home for a gourmet supper."

Very slowly, Jacques made a circuit of the desk. "There are times when I really don't like what I am," he said. "Or should I say what I'm supposed to be. And I sure as hell don't like what you just suggested."

"Hey!" Rita jerked down her jacket. "Don't get mad at me because you've got some kind of an itch that needs scratching and —"

"Cut it, Rita. You don't know what you're talking about. I've finally met a woman with some depth and I don't intend to miss an opportunity to get to know her better." Too bad a kid came with the package, but he'd figure out a way to win her over. "Gaby McGregor is one of a kind. She's got a lovely little girl named Mae."

"What?" Rita's mouth remained open. "A kid! You don't like kids."

"I damn well do like kids. I love kids."

"Since when?"

"Since —" Since never, but he could learn. "This is a very bright child with a wonderful vocabulary and a good sense of humor." La Place had been there since before he was born, which made the house "real old." Great sense of humor.

Rita shook her head and began shoveling the candy back into its crate. "We've got to get you back to civilization."

"Do you know, I actually feel *possessive* about Gaby." He laughed self-consciously. "Can you believe that?"

"I can't believe any of this."

"I'm making progress, y'know. She's not nearly as cool toward me as when we first met."

"Oh, good." The crate flaps smacked shut. "I only wish I could feel as enthusiastic about something in this dump of a town. Maybe I should work on developing an interest in fruit trees."

Jacques regarded her seriously. "Is something wrong, Rita?"

"Nothing."

He approached and bent to look into her face. "Yes there is. Forgive me. I've been too preoccupied with what's going on in my own life. Come on. Spill it."

"Nothing . . ." She stepped back and raised her chin. "Yes, there is. I hate this place and I hate the dense local yokels who live here. And most of all I *hate* being Bart Stanly's gofer. There. You asked and now you know."

"You aren't Bart's gofer," he said slowly. "You and Bart have different functions and you're at the same level."

"Tell him that, why don't you?" Her face grew pale, and freckles Jacques had never noticed before stood out on a nice nose. "He treats me like a slave. Get this. Do that. And I have to listen to every little idea he comes up with. Then I'm supposed to be over the moon about how brilliant he is."

"Rita —"

"He's driving me mad!" To Jacques's horror, huge tears welled in her eyes.

"Now, now." Awkwardly he patted her shoulder. "You're overwrought. Take a day off."

"And do what?" she almost screamed. "Watch the grass turn browner?"

Jacques cleared his throat. "I'll think of something." He pulled a tissue from a box and pressed it into her hand. "And I'll talk to Bart —"

"No! No." Sniffing, Rita dabbed at her eyes. "Don't do that, please. I can deal with Bart."

"You sure?"

"Absolutely." She gave him a watery smile. "Forget I said anything. I've had a difficult few days. Bart's okay most of the time."

Jacques watched her assessingly. Perhaps the lady protested too much. Maybe the real problem here was denial of feelings quite different from those Rita had declared for her colleague.

What he had to deal with, and now, was the next step in getting closer to Gaby. "Women like being courted, don't they?"

Rita looked blank.

"I mean, despite all the talk about equality, women like the gentle, romantic approach." Why hadn't he thought of this sooner? "Flowers, champagne. Soft music."

"Candy," Rita said and laughed.

Jacques bared his teeth. "I'll let that pass. I feel . . . euphoric. Yes, that's it. I could have something really fresh and satisfying with Gaby, I know I could."

"Fresh and satisfying?" Skepticism loaded Rita's voice.

"That's what I said and that's what I think." Heavy footsteps thudded on the wooden stairs, and the top of Bart's blond head came into view. "And here's the man himself. He must have followed his burning ears."

"Shush," Rita said urgently.

"Trust me." Jacques smiled an evil smile. "I'm feeling in a really good mood. She likes me. I can feel it and I like the feeling."

"Who likes you?" Bart's face resembled a week's worth of bad news.

Jacques decided to ignore the thunderous countenance. He felt too optimistic to be brought down by either Rita or Bart's foul tempers. "Gaby McGregor, of course. Don't tell me that's any surprise."

"I was afraid you'd say that." Bart dropped into a chair, stretched out his legs and let his feet flop apart. "Hi, Rita, love. How's it goin'?"

"Fine, not that you care."

There was definitely something odd between these two. "Why would you be afraid?"

"I ran into Camilla Roberts. She wants to see you. Says she's just passing through. I thought it might be a good idea to put her off until I'd warned you."

"Damn it." Camilla had been a nuisance for longer than Jacques wanted to remember. "Keep her out of my way for as long as you can. I want to get a shipment of fresh roses sent in."

Bart frowned up at him. "Am I allowed to ask why?"

"Sure. I'm going to snow Gaby with attention. Make them those red roses with frosty white inside the petals. Several dozen. Twelve dozen should do it. Long-stemmed. Baccarat crystal vases, one for each dozen. I want them here by tomorrow."

"Twelve dozen roses and twelve Baccarat vases." Bart scrubbed at his eyes and pinched the bridge of his nose. "Hell, what a mess."

Jacques dropped his hands to his sides.

"Would you like to elaborate on that re-mark?"

"Not if I could help it."

"Give it your best shot."

"You've decided to woo the fair Gaby, cor-rect?"

"Correct. For the first time in my life I've met a woman I think might actually be worth the effort."

"Sex and intellect all rolled up in one package."

"I wouldn't have put it quite like that, but close." Today, he resented having to deal with other people's jaded views. "We don't have to get into a discussion on this subject. Just arrange for the roses to be delivered to me. I'll take them to her myself."

"There's something you ought to know," Bart said into his fist.

"Have you noticed who raises pigs around here?"

"Pigs?" Bart and Rita chorused.

"Forget it." They'd never understand that he felt spontaneous and free — and ready to do the outrageous.

Bart got slowly to his feet. "I'm out of here. Let me know when you're ready to listen to me."

"Okay. I'm ready. I'm listening now."

"You're going to hate this."

Jacques sat on the edge of the desk. "*Tell* me."

"You think you've got a thing for Gaby McGregor?"

He hated the indirect approach. "I don't think, I know. And I'm going all out to make her see that she feels the same way."

Bart shifted. "You believe she does?"

"I'm sure of it."

"At this moment Gaby's out collecting signatures on a petition."

Jacques grinned, imagining black hair flipping in the breeze . . . and soft cotton shifting over even softer skin. "Gaby's never going to be idle. What cause is she championing?"

"The anti-Jacques Ledan cause. Gaby's doing her damnedest to get you run out of this town . . . for good."

9

Six foot plus of dark, powerfully lean — and evidently mean — muscle came into view and it was heading straight for Gaby.

"Thanks, Mrs. Meaker," she said hastily and tucked the clipboard under her arm. "You won't regret it." Goldstrike's postmistress nodded and went on her way.

Jacques had called last night and she'd hung up on him — five times. This morning she'd left home early to see how many signatures she could get before going to the shop. After deciding to dedicate yesterday to helping kick off the campaign, she felt anxious to get back to work.

"Gaby!"

He didn't sound any less angry than he had last night. Ducking her head and pretending to concentrate on keeping her hat in place, she scuttled past Caleb's gas station and whipped around the corner in the direction of Hacienda Heaven.

"Gaby!"

She slowed her pace. If this was going to be the moment of direct confrontation, so be it.

"War, huh?" He fell in beside her. "Are we going to talk about this?"

Gaby switched the clipboard to her other arm. "Not if I can help it."

"You can't help it." Looking straight ahead, a brown sack clasped in one hand, he strode purposefully at her side. "What did I do?"

"There's nothing to discuss, Jacques. Please excuse me."

Nigel Parker lounged in front of his hardware store. Gaby marched up to him and proffered the clipboard. "Good morning, Nigel. We're collecting signatures for a petition to block the project proposed by Ledan Enterprises."

"Well, now." Nigel straightened his long, rangy body and peered at the paper. "I don't rightly know how I feel about this."

"Good for you!" Jacques grabbed Nigel's hand and pumped. "That's what I like to see. A man with vision. You've been here in Goldstrike a long time, haven't you, sir?"

Nigel rolled a wad of chew from one cheek to the other. "Sure have. My dad was here before me, too. And his dad. My great-granddad settled here when they were still scrabbling for gold in them hills." He laughed and coughed.

"I love hearing the old stories," Gaby told him, sliding Jacques a withering glance. "Your family, and people like them, made Goldstrike what it is."

"What it *was*," Jacques remarked, centering his gaze on the hills. "They were men of vision. They had the guts to forge into a new frontier and take chances. Damn big chances they were, too."

Nigel nodded. "That's tellin' it."

"They were men who would have known what to do today," Jacques continued. "Nigel, if your great-grandfather were here today, he'd say that you come from stock that's never been afraid of something new. He'd tell you Goldstrike needs something new right now if it's not going to die. And he'd say, 'Nigel, this Ledan guy's got what you need. Support him.' That's what he'd want you to do."

He was completely unscrupulous. "Sign," Gaby said briskly, handing Nigel the pen. "Your great-grandfather would have signed and he'd want you to sign now. He wouldn't have wanted the town he founded to change into something that'll look like a fairground."

Jacques reached into the brown sack he carried and produced several gold-wrapped candies shaped like little pots and tied around with rainbow-colored ribbon. "Try these," he said, and gave them to Nigel. "We're making pots of gold the motto for Ledan Park in Goldstrike."

"Leprechaunville," Gaby muttered. "You'll never win."

"All's fair," Jacques murmured back. He

heaped more candy upon Nigel. "Your great-grandfather's gold — the gold he tore out of cruel rock, with little more than his bare hands, is what inspired our theme. Give some of these to your friends and tell them Jacques Ledan is looking forward to working with them — hand in hand — to make this town everything it can be."

Nigel considered the candy for a long time before leveling a brown stare on Jacques. "My great-granddaddy never did mine no gold. Didn't hold with it. He was an undertaker. Reckoned as how the kind of fools who wasted everythin' they had on hackin' away at dumb rocks weren't about to be long for this world. He figured there'd be more call for prettyin' up the remains and buryin' than marryin'. That's what he did afore he come out here. Ran a marryin' chapel."

Gaby pressed fingers to her mouth and swallowed a laugh. Jacques's arched brows slowly rose. "Your great-grandfather was a minister?" he asked.

"Nope. Thanks for the candy, though." Nigel took the pen from Gaby and signed the petition. "There. Now I guess everybody's happy. I'd better be gettin' on."

With Jacques at her side, Gaby watched Nigel go inside his store.

"The man's a moron," Jacques said. "*Everyone's* happy? What is that?"

"That's simplicity," Gaby told him. "We

131

aren't complicated people here."

"You aren't one of these people."

"I certainly am." A trace of discomfort crept up her spine. "What makes you think I'm not?" She couldn't expect to keep her origins from him indefinitely.

"No one told me. I'm not a fool. Don't ask me how, but you've managed to soak up some sophistication from somewhere and it shows."

She wished she could regard that as a compliment. "Well, have a good day."

A long, strong hand closed on her arm. "I've been trying to talk to you since yesterday morning. How come you didn't go to work all day?"

"I don't have to answer your questions."

"Why did you keep hanging up on me last night?"

He didn't know how to quit. "I didn't want to talk to you."

"I want to talk to you."

"Goodbye, Jacques." She turned away, but he didn't release her. "Let me go, please."

"I'm not hurting you."

"I didn't say you were."

"Please could we talk?" His voice became softer.

"About what?"

He spun her toward him. "About this foolishness! What happened since the last time we were together? I thought we were really getting somewhere."

"You thought you'd snowed me onto your side, you mean." She raised her chin and glared into his eyes — blue eyes turned almost black by frustration. "Admit it. You thought winning over the dumb little lady from the hat factory would be a cinch. Well, you were wrong. Now. Get out of my way."

"Gaby, I never thought any such thing. What I intend for you and me has nothing to do with what you do or what I do. We're going to have something special. You know that as well as I do."

His sharp cheekbones accentuated the lean lines of his face, the face of a hunter, a man who went after and got what he wanted.

"I think you'd better tell me what it is we're supposed to be going to have," Gaby said.

"You're being difficult." He pulled her close until she had to tip back her head to look at him. "We're going to be lovers."

Before she could stop herself, Gaby gasped. "Don't say things like that." She looked around. "Not here."

"We're both over twenty-one. What we choose to do with our personal lives is our own affair."

"*Don't* use that word!"

He smiled and slid his arm all the way around her. "*Affair?* It does have . . . an intimate ring. I rather like it, myself. We're going to make long, wonderful, sexy love, Gaby.

You and I are going to be addicted to the things we do together. I promise you that, and I don't promise anything I don't intend to carry out."

"Let me go," she said between gritted teeth. "Or I'll scream."

Jacques's response was to sweep off her hat and layer her against his muscular chest until she knew he would feel every tingling millimeter of her breasts through the orange silk blouse she wore. She felt her own flesh, its quickening, in a searing flash all the way to her knees.

"Gaby, Gaby." His fingertips moved lightly up and down her back. "I've been waiting for you a long time."

The fight seeped out of Gaby. She rested her forehead on his chest, at the opening of his khaki shirt where dark hair curled, and closed her eyes.

"It's like that for you, too, isn't it?" Jacques stroked her hair.

Gaby struggled against the desire to wrap her arms around him. "I don't have the faintest idea what you're talking about. You wear me out. I'm tired of arguing." She actually felt her body grow heavier. If he *weren't* holding her she'd be inclined to sit down right where she was.

"We don't have to argue. We have better things to do — like getting to know each other."

Like giving him a chance to lull her away from gathering signatures. "I'm going to go now, Jacques," she said carefully, planting her free hand in the middle of his chest and pushing herself away. "And I don't want you to interfere with what I'm doing again." His scent — clean, male skin and something very faintly woodsy — lingered.

"You don't want me to get out of Goldstrike."

"I . . ." She wanted to stay exactly where she'd just been — wrapped in his strong arms, against his solid chest, with her face nestled close enough to taste him if she felt like it. "We're going to fight you, Jacques."

"You don't sound convincing."

Camilla Roberts's face flashed before Gaby. "You're very good at turning women into slaves, aren't you?"

He laughed and fanned her face with her black straw hat. "What would make you say a thing like that?"

"Yesterday I had the dubious pleasure of meeting a true Jacques Ledan fan."

"One of many," he said, still chuckling.

"She said you were a visionary. The very word you used to try and flatter poor Nigel into your corner."

Jacques's smile slid. "Who are we talking about?"

"We're talking about the woman you were probably with last night. The one you must have tucked away somewhere while you kept bothering me on the phone."

Complete confusion settled on his face. "I don't know what you're talking about."

"Does the name Camilla Roberts ring a bell? She talked about you with pure diamond-studded stars in her eyes. She just *knew* you intended to offer her a piece of the action at the *spa!* This is all unbelievable."

"Gaby —"

"No. Don't try to explain or gloss any of this over." How could she, even for a second, forget what this man wanted from Goldstrike — and from her. "You can't use me, Jacques."

She cut around him and set off purposefully for Hacienda Heaven. When Jacques didn't follow she fought the temptation to look back. She didn't want him. *She didn't.*

Hacienda Heaven was separated from the road by a cracked parking lot fronted by a brick wall. A planting strip sported dusty plastic cacti alternated with molded pink flamingoes on poles.

Gaby reached the door of what had, during late mining days, been the site of a Chinese joss house. Barney's neon *Hablamos Español* sign flashed in double-time.

"Do they?" a male voice asked softly.

Gaby jumped and stepped back onto Jacques's feet. "Do they what?" she almost shrieked.

136

He nodded to the sign. "Speak Spanish."

"Yes . . . no. At least, I don't think so." She pushed the door.

"Thirsty?"

"I beg your pardon?"

This time he indicated Barney's other sign, this one hand-painted on a window amid a smattering of unlikely renditions of sombreros and large flowers. "Little early for some of the *frio cerveza*, isn't it?"

"If I was a drinking woman, Jacques Ledan, I'd be more than ready for a cold drink, or two, of beer or anything else." She shoved the door once more. It didn't budge.

"The place is closed."

"Observant of you."

"I could have told you the guy who owns the place isn't in."

Gaby narrowed her eyes. "How?" She started back the way she'd come.

"He drives a beaten-up green van." Jacques fell into an easy lope beside her. "You ought to watch that temper of yours. Gets in the way of optimum performance. One old, green van drove away while you were steaming up to the door. You'd have seen it if you hadn't been giving in to unfounded anger."

"I'm not angry."

"You're angry because you're jealous. Giving in to jealousy makes you feel out of control — which you are in this case — and

137

you're a very controlling personality."

They passed Nigel's store and reached Caleb's place on the corner of Main Street. "So far you haven't made any points with me this morning, Jacques. In fact, you've lost some."

"You're jealous because you want me, and you're afraid Camilla Roberts has beaten you to it."

Gaby rounded on him, opened her mouth, then closed it again firmly and turned left toward her workroom. The man was bored. Nothing more. Of course an argument could be made that if he truly believed he needed her on his side, he wouldn't try to alienate her. But then, he might think this pseudo-smitten act would be enough to flatter a dumb little hick hat maker into infatuated submission. On the other hand, he was powerful enough not to have to run around doing his own dirty work.

"I've known Camilla a long time."

"Lucky you."

"Please, Gaby. Listen to me. She is absolutely nothing to me and never was. A hanger-on at parties I've given — that's it."

"I'll bet you give lots of parties and I don't see you as a man who's ever without a gaggle of what you call hangers-on. I'm going to work now. The war is still on."

He stopped and turned up his palms. "Okay, have it your way. See you later."

Frowning, Gaby watched him stroll away

before walking slowly to the courtyard behind the workroom.

Char, working alone on one of the pieces for *Going to the Dogs*, greeted Gaby with a cheerful, "Hiya, toots."

"That is one very strange man," Gaby said. "First he follows me all over town while I tell him to get lost. Then he just gives up and walks off."

"The romance blossoms," Char said, tacking ostrich plumes to a chartreuse felt tricorn.

Gaby ignored the comment. "Why would he suddenly decide not to fight anymore?"

"You just said you told him to get lost."

"Yes, but . . ." Gaby put down the clipboard. She didn't want him to stay, but she didn't want him to go. "Good grief, was that the shop bell?"

"Certainly was." The plumes were deep blue and turquoise dusted with silver. "Any idea who it might be before nine on a weekday morning?"

"You go."

"Impossible. We don't have any time to waste on this project and I seem to be the only one working on it."

From the shop came a whistled version of "Somewhere Over the Rainbow." "Char," Gaby whispered hoarsely. "It's *him*. Take it from me — he won't go away unless you go and tell him to."

139

"Nothing doing." Char smiled sweetly. "Tell him yourself. I'll send help if you don't come back in, oh, an hour?"

"This isn't funny," Gaby wailed.

The shop bell rang again. Then silence.

"He's gone," Gaby said. Why wasn't she relieved?

The bell sounded once more.

Char set down the hat. "What —"

And again the tinny noise trilled. "Maybe the door isn't properly shut," Gaby said.

"The wind could be catching it," Char added, but made no move to check. The bell rang again, and again. She held up her fingers and counted silently. "Would that be in or out?"

Gaby screwed up her eyes. "In or out?"

"If it isn't the wind. There can't be *that* many customers lined up in the shop."

Another ring.

"You *have* to go," Gaby said.

"It could be a kid just opening and closing the door for the hell of it."

"Hello!" A familiar male voice echoed along the passageway from the shop. "Gaby? You forgot something."

She pressed her hands to her middle and whispered, "I'm going to have to face him, aren't I?"

Char picked up an ostrich feather and nodded. "The sooner the better."

With a final glare in her assistant's direction, Gaby marched from the workroom and into the shop . . . and stopped.

"You forgot your hat," Jacques said, holding it out.

Gaby glanced briefly at him, then she stared at an amazing display of roses in crystal vases that caught sunlight through the windows. "Where did those come from?" Prisms of colored light flashed from the crystal.

"I brought them."

Dozens and dozens of red roses with frosty white centers. "Why?"

"Take your hat. Hats look very good on you. Have I told you that?"

"No," she said shortly, taking the black straw and tossing it onto a head form. "Thanks."

A scuffing noise heralded Char's appearance. "I need to step out and —" She stopped in midsentence and her mouth remained open. "Wow. Are we opening a florist's shop?"

"They're a gift for Gaby," Jacques said. "You must be Char. Mae mentioned you."

"She did?" Char came farther into the shop and appeared even more entranced by Jacques than the roses. "Mae's a great little girl. I never had kids, but if I had I'd have wanted them to be just like her."

"Bright," Jacques said, bestowing a dazzling smile — the kind of bone-to-jelly smile only he could bestow — upon Char. "And a pretty thing, too. Like her mother."

Gaby swallowed and willed away any blush that might be marshaling forces. She failed. Her face throbbed.

"Yes," Char said and sat on the black cane chair. "Gaby is beautiful, isn't she? Everyone thinks so. I never met a red-blooded man who could look at Gaby and not want . . . well, we both know what I mean."

"We certainly do," Jacques agreed, turning his attention to Gaby. The smile softened, became lazy, sensual. "Gaby already knows what *I* want."

This was *too* much. "Why did you bring all these?" She swept a hand in the direction of the roses. "Why? I thought you were angry with me."

"I ordered the roses before you decided to make a career out of disagreeing with me."

Gaby snorted. "Naturally. You wouldn't buy roses for someone who didn't agree with you, would you?"

"You bet I wouldn't." His mouth tightened into a tough line.

"You're the kind of man who brings roses home to his wife when he wants something."

"Does that have a particular meaning?" he asked, so sweetly she smarted.

"You know what I mean."

"Tell me."

"Sex," Char announced. "She means that some men bring incentives —"

"Char!" Gaby turned her back on both of them.

A scuffling followed. "Well," Char said. "If you don't need me for a while . . . See you shortly."

Gaby listened to Char's departing footsteps with something like dread. The silence that closed in felt electrically sharp.

Jacques cleared his throat. "I want you to have the roses, Gaby."

"I'm sorry you wasted your money."

"Couldn't we try to start over?"

She faced him.

"Let's put all the hard feelings behind us," he said. "I think I know what's bothering you and I've already thought of a way to put it right."

When he looked like that: sincere, intensely concerned and good-looking enough to melt the soles of her feet, Gaby couldn't hold on to her irritation. "What do you think is bothering me?" He understood, actually comprehended that she was hesitant to let go with him because —

"You're ambitious in your way," Jacques said. "It's been wrong of me to assume that because you're in business in a very small way and in a place like Goldstrike, you

143

don't want to be successful."

Disappointment outweighed frustration — almost.

Jacques crossed his arms. "If I'd been paying enough attention I'd have realized that your competitiveness is one of the things that attracts me to you. You're a strong woman."

She had no idea where this was heading.

"The contract to make baseball caps must be a big deal to you. I should be able to put myself in your place and see how big. Will you forgive me on that one?"

Gaby couldn't form a single word.

Jacques nodded and bowed his head. "I knew you were the kind of woman who didn't bear grudges. The point is — and I see it now — that you don't like the idea of doing the preliminary work, then watching it taken out of your hands when the demand gets really big. Am I right?"

"A man of vision," she said, very softly.

For an instant he appeared baffled. Then he grinned. "Subtle. That's something else I like — your sense of humor. Anyway, I've worked it all out. It must be as obvious to you as it is to me that you won't be able to handle the mass production past a certain stage. Am I right?"

Fascinated, Gaby nodded slowly.

"Right. But that isn't going to matter because there's a way for you to go right on getting a good, big piece of the action."

"And everyone wants a piece of your action," Gaby said, almost to herself. Camilla Roberts's face flashed again. "That must get quite tiresome."

Jacques shrugged. "That's business."

Which, by extension, meant that she was just business — with the added possibility of a few fringe benefits for Jacques Ledan.

"Don't give any of this another thought. I'm going to take care of you. Can you guess how?"

Gaby shook her head.

"You're going to become the exclusive outlet for Go for the Gold in Goldstrike souvenirs. Right here in this little shop." Enthusiasm radiated from his broad gesture. "Gaby, not one GFTG rain poncho, GFTG stuffed animal, coloring book or T-shirt . . . and certainly not one baseball cap will ever be sold that doesn't come from Gaby's little shop!"

She shook her head again, very, very slowly. "You're kidding."

"I knew this was the answer." He pulled a rose from its vase and handed it to Gaby. "Here's to a great partnership. We're going to paint that logo right on your window — Go for the Gold in Goldstrike. Official Souvenir Outlet."

Gaby remembered to breathe again. "And

there'll be a rainbow, of course," she croaked.

"That's the girl! The biggest rainbow you ever saw."

10

Far below, on the road winding through the hills toward La Place, a brief flash of light pierced the gray afternoon.

Slouched in his favorite chair near the study windows, Jacques let his newspaper fall to the floor. A heavy sky pressed down upon the hilltops as far as he could see, yet a break in the cloud had allowed sunlight to catch a car windshield.

"You aren't going to believe this," Bart had told him on the phone, sounding excited. "Stay put until I get there."

Jacques had no doubt it was Bart's Porsche that approached. The road ended at La Place and no one else was expected. The prospect of a dose of Stanly enthusiasm sent Jacques's already sagging mood earthward.

There were times when a man deserved to be alone with his depression.

Gaby had told him to go to hell. "There's the door," had been her exact words.

And he'd been so reasonable.

And she'd thrown his understanding and generosity in his face . . . with no explanation.

He got up and stood close to the glass. The study, cantilevered from the back of the main house, overhung a steep hillside cloaked with blue oaks.

Gaby would like this house — maybe even more than he did. "Black Jacques" had been the nickname of his twenties, and the notion that he was silent, dark and complicated hung on in some quarters. No one really knew him, damn it. Sure he could be difficult, but at some levels he was traditional, conservative even. Gaby McGregor could never, under any circumstances, be described as traditional or conservative.

That's why she'd like La Place more than he did — if he could ever get her here. This house *deserved* a woman who appreciated the spectacularly unusual.

Gaby and the word spectacular fitted together perfectly.

What the hell *did* she want from him?

He confronted the issue he'd been skirting: what did *he* want from her?

Loud barking from the other side of the house meant his dog had heard the distant approach of an engine.

Jacques buttoned his trailing denim shirt and set off through corridors lined with blond paneling all the way to vaulted ceilings.

Spike — all fifteen pounds of her — took one look at Jacques and subsided into a doleful, dark-eyed heap on the floor by the front door.

"That's the girl," Jacques said. "We understand each other perfectly, don't we?"

Spike heaved a huge sigh. A mutt with gray fur, skinny legs and a tail like a battle flag, the dog's most endearing quality was an unerring ability to judge her master's moods . . . and adopt them.

Jacques opened the door as the silver Porsche swung into a circular courtyard built at the center of the buildings comprising La Place.

The car shot around the fountains with Bart's customary reckless style and slid to a halt. The passenger door opened to reveal Rita, dressed for a Saturday afternoon in a basic black jumpsuit.

"Boy, are you going to hate this," she said, an expression of deep gloom on her face.

Bart arrived beside her before she could stand up. "We made an agreement, sweetheart," he said, gallantly offering a hand. "I do the subject lead-in and you clean up as necessary. Right?"

She ignored his hand and emerged to stand in front of Jacques. "Right. But, boy, are you going to hate this, Jacques."

"Great," he said, standing back to let her pass. "I can hardly wait."

Bart slapped Jacques on the back, shot him a sympathetic grimace and followed Rita into the house.

Whining softly, Spike fell in at Jacques's heel.

Rita marched directly into the sun room and settled herself in a swinging rattan chair suspended from a crossbeam. "Why is that animal moaning?" she asked, eyeing the culprit with disdain.

Jacques stooped and Spike vaulted into his arms. "She's very sensitive — like me."

"Let's get this over with," Rita said to Bart, studying apparently perfect fingernails. "The sooner he knows, the sooner we'll know just how much damage we'll need to patch up."

"You promised you'd let me do this, sweetheart."

Jacques looked from Bart to Rita, expecting her to tell her supposed rival to cut out the "sweethearts" and quit telling her what to do.

"Sorry, Bart," Rita said with a smile. "I won't say another word."

"Sorry, Bart," Jacques murmured under his breath. Why should he expect to understand anything about the people he paid a fortune to work for him?

"Napoleon Paradise made contact."

"When?" Jacques kicked the door shut behind him, his attention riveted on Bart. "How?"

"This morning. By fax."

"Why the hell didn't you tell me on the phone?"

"Because —" Rita started to explain.

"Rita!" Bart cut her off. "He's coming. That's all that matters."

A deep edge of excitement sent Jacques pacing beside lush green and flowering plants that lined the almost totally glass room. "When will he be here?"

"Sometime next week. They'll contact us with final instructions. You know how it is with Napoleon."

"The man's crazy," Rita said dispassionately.

"He's also brilliant," Jacques reminded her. "He's the one man who can design a theme park the whole world will clamor to visit. If he wants to come here in some sort of hermetically sealed pod — in the dead of night — with a platoon of armed guards, so be it."

"Bart, *tell* him."

"*Okay*, Rita. Let me do this my own way and in my own time."

Jacques stopped pacing. "Tell me what? Is there going to be some glitch with this? You know how much we've got riding on the park."

Bart had remained standing. Now he approached Jacques, appeared about to say something, but went to examine a particularly lush hanging fern instead. "How do you stand being all alone in this place?"

"I like my own company." Not strictly true — at least not at the moment.

"No one with a home this size goes without live-in staff."

"I go without because I prefer it that way. All the help I need, I get. What did you come here to tell me?"

Bart continued to examine plants while Rita swung.

Jacques waited until he couldn't stand the silence any longer. "Let's have it, Bart. *Now.*"

"Nice fern."

"Bart."

"Yeah, well. Okay. Ever heard of a guy by the name of Michael Copeland?"

Jacques furrowed his brow. "Does he work for Napoleon?"

"Forget Napoleon," Rita snapped, stilling her chair by applying a toe to the ground. "Napoleon's coming. We don't know exactly when as yet. You'll know as soon as we do. Just get on with it, Bart."

"Copeland's a theatrical costume designer. Works primarily in the movies now."

"Copeland." Jacques shook his head. "Copeland . . . yes, yes. Oscar for best costumes about three years ago?"

"That's the guy," Bart said.

"He's Gaby McGregor's husband," Rita added, intent now on the leaden sky that crowded down on the sun room's glass roof.

For seconds Jacques stared at Rita. "Her ex-husband, you mean," he said finally. "She's divorced."

"Uh-huh," Bart said. "Divorced for seven years. One daughter, Mae, seven years old. Seems Mr. Copeland wasn't keen on the white picket fence and nursery routine. The marriage fell apart while Gaby was pregnant."

Jacques turned away. "Creep," he said through his teeth. What kind of man abandoned his wife while she was expecting his child?

"Evidently that was the opinion of most people who knew them. Apparently Gaby defends Copeland. Says he never wanted kids and she knew it."

"How do you know all this?"

"Her assistant — Char Brown — was in when we stopped by earlier," Rita said. "Evidently she's the surrogate grandma figure to the kid. I asked a couple of leading questions about her boss and got what has to be the party line — Gaby doesn't blame her ex for what happened."

"That doesn't alter a damn thing and you know it. A man who *is* a man doesn't walk away from a pregnant wife."

An awkward silence followed, broken by the sound of Bart clearing his throat.

"Copeland's still a big shot in LA, isn't he?" Jacques ventured.

"He sure is," Rita said. "Have you heard of a movie musical called *Going to the Dogs*?"

"Hasn't everyone? It's supposedly going to be next year's big box-office hit. Is Copeland doing the costumes?"

After a missed beat, Bart said, "Yes."

"God," Jacques said. "And while he rolls in glory and bucks, his wife and daughter grub along in a backwater trying to make ends meet on the proceeds from a hat factory!"

"Jacques —"

"No wonder she didn't fall over herself to accept my offer yesterday —"

"Jacques —"

"She must have seen me as another man on the make," Jacques said, interrupting Bart. "Poor little thing. I stood there making grandiose offers about her becoming the exclusive concession outlet for GFTG souvenirs. She was probably remembering her schmuck of an ex-husband standing at the altar and promising to share everything he had with her, then walking away when she needed him most."

"What do promises at the altar have to do with any of this?" Rita asked, leaning forward.

Jacques spread his hands. "Well . . . it's subtle. You've got to be able to make the leap and see it through her eyes. I'm going to go and apologize."

"For what?" Bart stuffed his hands in his pockets. "You aren't responsible for Copeland's behavior."

"I'm responsible for not making the effort

154

to find out more about Gaby."

"And how."

He looked sharply at Rita. "What does that mean?"

"Poor little Gaby isn't poor little Gaby."

"Explain that."

Frowning with concentration, she wound the chains that supported her chair around and around.

"Rita?"

"I'm not surprised she's hesitant to explain," Bart said. "If anyone should have known, it's Rita."

"Me?" She lifted her toe from the floor and spun wildly.

Bart grabbed the spiraling chair and jerked the whole contraption to a halt. "You." He tipped her to stand in front of him. "Jacques and I don't *wear* hats."

"Neither do I!"

"You're a woman."

"So?"

"So, women know about those things. You blew it, Rita."

"Hey, hey." Insinuating himself between them, Jacques crossed his arms. "Never mind who should have told what. Just tell me what all this is about — now — with no more side trips."

Rita and Bart looked at each other with raised brows.

"Gaby is *the* Gaby," Bart said at last. "You

know, *the* hat Gaby? Milliner to anyone who *is* anyone. A few first ladies, the odd dozen or so female ambassadors or ambassadors' wives, those nothing little people at the Academy Awards I think we mentioned — and on, and on."

Jacques slowly put Spike down. "That's not possible."

"That's what we thought," Rita said. "It was Camilla Roberts — by the way, she's still holed up in my trailer. I don't know how much longer I can put her off from coming up here to find you — but Camilla made the connection between Gaby and *the* Gaby."

"For God's sake stop calling her *the* Gaby." A deep, burning agitation made itself felt. "She runs a . . . hat . . ." The agitation caught fire. "Finish your story. *Now!*"

Amazingly, Bart put what appeared to be a protective arm around Rita's shoulders. "This isn't any more our fault than yours."

"I pay you to make sure I know everything about everyone who might be important to me. Get on with it."

"We're trying to." Rita shrugged free of Bart's arm. "Gaby McGregor is and has been for some time, a world-famous milliner. Seven years ago, after her divorce — for reasons we haven't quite determined — she decided to run her business from Goldstrike.

"By the way, as we speak, Ms. McGregor is under contract to her ex-husband to produce the hats that will be worn in *Going to the Dogs*. All the characters will wear hats."

A nerve twitched beside Jacques's left eye. "I see," he said softly. He unzipped and unsnapped his jeans, shoved his shirt inside, rezipped and resnapped. "Very, very funny. I hope she's had lots of fun, because now it's going to be my turn."

"Jacques." Rita caught his forearm. "None of us gave the woman a chance to say who she was."

"And she didn't bother to enlighten us," Jacques said. "She's at her house, did you say?"

"No. Losers' Ridge."

He paused on his way to the door. "What the hell is she doing at Losers' Ridge?"

"Char Brown said Gaby borrows a horse and rides there pretty frequently. The kid's in Los Angeles with Copeland for a week."

Jacques didn't bother to question why the supposed reluctant father would want his daughter with him. "Get back to town and make sure everything's set for Napoleon Paradise." He strode from the room.

"What are you going to do?" Rita asked, trotting in his wake.

"Take a trip to Losers' Ridge," he told her. "Gaby McGregor's about to learn a lesson."

11

Jacques Ledan wasn't the type of man who forgave and forgot.

But since their encounters were likely to be of the briefest kind in future, there was almost zero chance that she'd ever know exactly how angry he might be at her rejection of him yesterday.

"Exclusive concession."

Gaby settled her rump more comfortably into the grassy dip she'd selected, drew up her knees and concentrated on staying mad at Mr. Ledan.

Arrogant SOB.

The good of Goldstrike was his mission and the reason for his being? He knew nothing about the town or the people who lived there. True, things had gotten tough, but the fix wouldn't be found in throwing away everything treasured and planting some hateful, plastic project in its place.

No one had ever kissed her as Jacques had.

They were beings from different planets, destined to disagree on anything and everything.

His every touch made her nerves stand up and beg for more.

A relationship built on the purely physical was doomed.

Hell, she wanted more of that kind of doom!

Clouds moved slowly, heavily, parting almost rhythmically to allow the sun's escape in brilliant shafts that warmed Gaby's back through her checked cotton shirt. Blinding white fog, subtly shaded with blue gray, filled the valley below Losers' Ridge the way a fickle burden of dry ice vapor might nuzzle a giant punch bowl. Gaby wrapped her arms around her legs. No one who hadn't seen this would believe that a northern California valley could look like a soft, visibly shifting glacier.

Vi, the docile old roan Gaby borrowed from time to time, whinnied softly. "Steady, girl," Gaby called without turning around. Vi belonged to one of the women who sometimes helped in the workroom.

The roan snorted, and rocks skittered from beneath her hoofs. "What's with you, Vi?"

Gaby looked over her shoulder directly into a shaft of sunshine. She squinted, and drew in a quick breath.

"Who — ?" She bit off the question. The identity of the man astride a silver Arabian wasn't in doubt. Shading her eyes, Gaby watched Jacques.

And, silently, he watched her.

The Arabian was magnificent: big, slender and one hundred percent unpredictable power.

So was the man.

Flipping the reins, Jacques shifted in the saddle and walked his mount a few steps downhill.

Still he didn't speak.

The sun faded and she dropped her hand. He wore a denim shirt — mostly open — and faded jeans that strained over long, strongly muscled legs. His brown boots were scuffed, his hair mussed . . . and his eyes were pure, dark blue ice.

"Hi." She swallowed and drew in her bottom lip.

The horse danced a little closer.

Jacques didn't smile, didn't respond. He hunched his wide shoulders and rested a wrist on the horn. Wind flirted with the animal's mane and flattened the man's shirt to his chest. Beneath the shirt, dark hair curled over tanned skin. She'd known he was a big man. But he'd never looked this big . . . or this angry.

Gaby felt her own temper thin. "Hello, Jacques. Off your beaten track, aren't you?"

He twitched the rein and, with the slightest pressure from his knees, urged the Arabian on. "You really don't have any way of knowing what is or isn't my beaten track." He looked directly down upon Gaby.

She shrugged, but her heart beat faster.

"I rode in these hills when I was a boy."

Annoyance straightened her back. "Really?" He truly thought that having visited the area all his life, as a spoiled rich kid, gave him deep understanding of the dynamics here.

"This isn't about me," he said.

"This?"

He edged even closer until she had to tip her head to see his face. "Does Mae like visiting her father?"

Now her stomach made an entire loop. "Yes, she does. How did you know that's where she was?"

"Why don't you blame Michael Copeland for leaving you while you were pregnant?"

If he'd punched her, she couldn't have felt more shocked.

"Mmm." His smile — tight, thin — driving those fascinating vertical grooves into his cheeks, didn't warm his eyes. "Did you really think I'd never find out who you are?"

Gaby bent forward and rubbed her brow. "You know who I am."

"What?"

She looked at him again. "You know who I am."

"I do now."

"You did before. Jacques —" scrambling, she got to her feet "— I guess I can understand you feeling a bit irritated. You aren't

161

used to surprises. Jacques Ledan controls his world, doesn't he?"

"Jacques Ledan doesn't play stupid games with people he cares about."

"Neither . . ." The next breath she took stayed in her throat. "What's that supposed to mean?"

"Forget it. You deliberately misled me."

"No." She burned under his gaze. "At least, not at first."

"You didn't need to do so at all, lady. I was straight with you."

"Why should you care?" she snapped. "All that mattered to you was getting what you want. You sashayed in here and told us all what we were going to do. Did you ever, even once, actually *ask* me if I wanted to make your damn baseball caps? Did you?"

"You're being unreasonable."

"Because I'm telling it like it is? Give me a break." Grabbing at his mount's bridle, she glared up at Jacques. "First you sent in your trained animals, then you showed in person with the big guns to tell me exactly what prizes you intended to shower upon me."

"And in between, you and I discovered something else about ourselves," he said in a soft, still voice that cut to Gaby's core. "Don't forget that. You sure as hell didn't fight me too hard."

"Okay. I admit that." Denying the truth wouldn't change it. "But I also admit I made a mistake in responding to you." Even though she ached to touch him again, to feel him touch her.

"You deliberately misled me."

"*You* tried to use me. First as some sort of cheap labor. Then as a direct line to the people of Goldstrike."

"I never tried to use you. God, but you must have laughed up your sleeve at me."

Gaby grasped his calf. "Why would I laugh at you? I didn't ask you to come here. None of us did." Beneath her fingers, his leg was steel hard.

"Don't tell me you didn't enjoy making an ass of me."

"*I* didn't make you that."

"In other words you think that's what I am, anyway." His leg flexed. "Damn it. I've made men pay for doing a whole lot less to me."

She crossed her arms and blinked at sudden, completely foreign tears. "I don't know why you're shouting at me — and threatening me."

"I never shout."

"*All right.* But you're used to getting your own way and you hate it that this time it's not going to happen."

He moved so quickly, Gaby had no time to react. Leaning from the saddle, Jacques shot an arm around her waist and hoisted her into the air.

"Stop it!" Kicking only made him tighten his grip. "Put me down!"

His laugh chilled her . . . and excited her. "You don't want me to stop, sweetheart. Oh, no. I've just decided what it was I came out here to do."

"Put me down!" Gaby screamed.

Jacques's response was to shift back and swing her to sit in front of him. "You know you don't want me to put you down," he said against her neck. "Up to now, the game has been yours, hasn't it? You've played with me and enjoyed every second. Now it's my turn to call the shots."

Her heart leapt. "I will *not* be manhandled." A wild wriggle only served to slide her bottom firmly between his legs. "I'm expected at home."

"I don't think so. Mae's with her daddy and you're out riding for the day." With one arm wrapped firmly around her, Jacques used his free hand — and the thighs that pressed Gaby's — to guide his horse back to Vi's side. He gathered the roan's rein. "There's a whole lot of this day left. We're not going to waste any of it. *Git,* Snake."

"Snake?" She tried to pry his hand loose, only to have him spread his fingers until the thumb met her breast. "Who would call a horse Snake?"

"The name came with him. He was a gift."

"Some gift."

164

Behind her, Jacques used the motion of his hips to secure their balance — and Snake's gait. And the motion reminded Gaby how hard a man could be, and how soft a woman was . . . and how they could complement each other.

She flushed all the way to her toes.

Snake broke into a gallop along the side of the ridge. "This is ridiculous," Gaby shouted, the words jarring from her throat. "Who do you think you are? The Red Shadow?"

He laughed and she felt the vibration. "Black Jacques to some, baby." Finding the spot on her neck he seemed to favor, he sang, "My Desert is Waiting," in a gravelly baritone just offkey enough to be charming — too charming.

Everything about him was exciting . . . intoxicating.

She dared not wriggle again. "I don't want to call you anything. These are hills, not sand dunes. Sane men don't sweep women onto their horses and carry them away."

"I promise I won't carry you far," Jacques said. "Just far enough to show you a place I'm fond of. I'm the only one who knows about it. We'll be safe there — and very private."

His implication hit home. Gaby clenched her stomach against the instant response he evoked. Damn it, she would not be swept off her feet . . . but she was . . . and enjoying it too much.

Spurring on Snake, Jacques maneuvered along a path to the top of the ridge.

Gaby felt every skillful jerk and switch in the rhythm of his body, and closed her eyes.

"Okay," she said, when they set off along the narrow spine of rocky land. "You've had your fun, Jacques. Time to pack up your toys and go home."

He laughed again. "I'm glad you agree."

She bit her lip, refusing to smile. "I walked into that one. I'm not a toy. And I don't play with anyone I don't want to play with."

"Then we don't have a problem. We both know you want to *play* with me."

Gaby tried to turn in the saddle. Immediately she knew her mistake. A large, long-fingered hand held her in place using the most obvious anchor — her right breast.

"Jacques, don't," she said through her teeth.

The smallest move and he found and slipped his thumb under the neck of her shirt and over the swell of flesh above her bra. "I'm open to negotiation," he said. "Where would you rather be alone with me? At La Place in the brand new hot tub I've just had built? It's open to the sky, Gaby. And it's warm in there — and very, very wet. I like wet, don't you?" The tip of his thumb grazed the top of her nipple.

She closed her eyes and leaned against him.

"Oh, Gaby, Gaby." Jacques brought his cheek against hers. "We aren't going to be able to hold out, sweetheart. You know that?"

"You're not being fair."

Very gently he rubbed his rough jaw back and forth over the soft skin of her cheek. "Sometimes being fair doesn't pay off. This is one of those times. Today I'm going to do what's wise. That means what pleases both of us the most."

"Wise? Or self-indulgent?"

"Then there's that secret place I mentioned. A stand of madrone that shelters a bed of grass so soft it feels like velvet. Smooth, Gaby — satin on silky skin." His hand was all the way inside the bra, cupping her breast.

"Jacques . . ." She couldn't think.

"Yes, sweetheart? Is that hot tub, or velvet grass?"

"I want . . . I want . . ."

"Oh, so do I. I want everything with you." Deftly he hooked Vi's rein over the horn. "We're alone out here, Gaby. You, me, the sky — and the wind." With sure fingers. Jacques slipped her shirt buttons from their holes.

"I ought to go." But she wouldn't.

"The madrones are closest," Jacques said,

and tugged her shirt from her jeans, down her shoulders and free of her wrists.

The wind he spoke of smote her hot cheeks — and her tingling body. "This is madness. I can't be out here half-naked."

"You aren't yet." She felt him work behind her to undo and remove his own shirt. "Relax. Play with me, Gaby. Let me be the leader."

They made an abrupt turn and started down the other side of the ridge. Snake's hoofs thudded evenly while Vi galloped valiantly behind.

Jacques folded his arms around Gaby, held her against warm, male skin and crisp hair, and tensed, flexible muscle. The horse gathered speed until Gaby's hair began to rip free of the long braid down her back. Layered on Jacques's chest, bare skin to bare skin, the wild mountain scents rushing in, she knew — for the first time since she'd first met and loved Michael — the sweetly shocking force of pure arousal.

"We're crazy," Gaby yelled. Her lungs expanded erratically. The thudding of the horses' hoofs thundered in her ears.

"Duck!" Jacques did the ducking for both of them, bending over Gaby, bowing to sweep beneath the tangled branches of madrones at the edge of a tree-filled gully.

Gaby laughed and batted at twigs that caught her hair. "Stop, you nut. Stop!"

He rode with the unerring certainty of a man who knew exactly where he was going. Incense cedar, its lacy leaves shivering, nudged ponderosa pines among the madrone.

As quickly as the little forest had enclosed them, a clearing appeared. Jacques hauled on Snake's reins and the horse reared.

Jacques quieted the animal and slid from his back. "Come on." His tanned skin gleamed and his teeth showed very white in a triumphant grin. "Come to me, Gaby." He tossed their shirts across the saddle and reached up to grasp her waist.

She looked down, unable to ignore her breasts, nude but for a wisp of a red bra more provocative than if she'd worn nothing. And she looked into Jacques's upturned face. Sensuality glinted in his midnight eyes, eyes that made a slow passage over her body before his grip tightened and he lifted her from the horse.

Holding her aloft, he brought her middle to his mouth and kissed her tensed skin, dipped his tongue beneath the waist of her jeans and into her navel.

"No." A spasm shot to her knees.

"No?" Slowly, he lowered her, let her slide down his length, tasted each fresh spot that passed his lips until her toes met soft grass. "I don't think you mean no." Looping his hands around her neck, Jacques tipped up her chin with his thumbs.

For what felt a very long time, he studied her face. "Tell me you want me?"

Her stomach fell away. "This doesn't feel like me," she told him weakly. "I've been so quiet for so long."

He snorted. "That's not a description I'd have used for you."

"I don't mean . . . I mean . . ."

"Ssh." He rested his mouth on her brow. "I wasn't thinking. You've been busy being Mae's mom, haven't you? Is that what you mean?"

She bit her trembling lip. "Uh-huh. All I wanted was to make a new life. A different life from the one I had. LA was never right for me."

"Too fast?"

"Too everything." And what was this — this moment that made her feel like an electrically charged being she hardly knew?

Jacques ran his hands down her shoulders and held her arms. "Are you saying you haven't . . . You were divorced seven years ago, Gaby."

"There hasn't been anyone for me since then," she told him simply. With one tentative finger, she traced his breast bone, and his ribs, first one, then another and another. "And Michael was the first. Prosaic, aren't I?"

"You don't look prosaic at this moment."

She felt him look at her breasts. "This can't be right, Jacques."

"Kiss me."

"I don't know much about you."

"Dull. A successful man who inherited his success."

"I don't think I believe that. Not entirely. Didn't you turn your success into more success, maybe?"

"Maybe. Let's not talk about candy. It bores me these days. Look at me."

Instead, Gaby stared steadfastly at his broad chest. "You have the kind of body that could make a liar out of me."

He laughed shortly. "Explain that?"

Spreading her fingertips, she feathered across his nipples, smiled at the ripple of tension that passed over him, and stroked his sides all the way to his waist and inside his jeans to knead his belly with her knuckles.

"God, Gaby," he gasped. "I asked for an explanation."

With a quick glance into his eyes, she pressed her breasts to his chest and moved slowly back and forth. The lace couldn't be stimulating him more than it did her. She shuddered and opened her mouth over one flat, male nipple. Carefully, she closed her teeth and flicked the tip of her tongue.

"Gaby!"

"I'm explaining," she breathed. "Your body is making me want a lot of things I haven't thought about in too long. You're beautiful, Jacques. All man. Sexy as hell. I'll never forget the first time I saw you."

"You'll never know what I thought when I first saw you." He was panting. His hands, crossed over her shoulderblades, opened and closed reflexively.

"Did you think you'd like to make love right there, on the floor, Jacques? Did you want to get inside me even then?"

"Don't." Grasping her unraveling pigtail, he pulled her face from him. Strain showed in every line of his face, every visible vein in his neck. "Yes. Yes, my quiet lady. I wanted you right then. But not the way I want you now."

Exhilaration flooded Gaby. Laughing, she wrenched away. "Tell me how you want me now."

"Come here." He grabbed for her but she eluded him. "You little tease."

Whirling, she managed to pull her hair from his fingers. "Tease? Me? I'm a hick, Jacques. A poor little country girl. See this country girl run."

"Don't do it, Gaby — don't."

She laughed back at him and ran, her feet flying over the shaded, springy turf, her heart beating so hard it caught in her throat.

"I warned you!"

Jacques made no sound, but Gaby knew he came after her. Panting, she glanced over her shoulder. "No!" She sprinted, wove between the trees, dodged.

"Got you!"

She came face to face with Jacques around the ridged trunk of an incense cedar — and screamed. "You don't have me!"

Swallowing great gulps of air, she faked and darted in the opposite direction.

This time she heard his breathing. Her yell squeaked to nothing.

"Oh, yes," Jacques ground out, leaping into her path. "Yes, dear lady."

And his fingers descended on her shoulder, slid as she twisted yet again, and hooked into the back of her bra.

The scrap of red material gave way in an instant. "Ah!" She clutched for the bra in vain. Jacques twirled her to face him and she staggered back, her breasts swinging free.

"Ah," Jacques echoed, running his gaze over her. "Ah, *yes*. You like it rough and tumble, huh?"

Gaby backed away, covering her breasts with her hands. "I'm sorry," she said, trembling now, unbearably excited now. "I shouldn't have run."

"I'm so glad you did."

He made a grab and caught her wrist, pulled her hand away. "Don't hide from me, Gaby. I won't let you, anyway."

Another step backward, and another. "We don't know each other. Not really," she said.

He tilted up his face and laughed at the treetops. "Very soon you and I are going to know each other as well as any man and woman ever could."

"I don't mean —"

"In the biblical sense? I did. I do. You're breathing hard, Gaby. D'you know what that does?"

She shook her head.

"It makes your wonderful breasts do things that aren't making it any easier to be inside these pants."

Outrageously she blushed.

Jacques laughed again. "I'm never going to get tired of you. Are you going to keep on backing away?"

"Yes."

"No you're not."

She walked into a tree.

"See." He spread his legs and trapped her hips, ground his hard, heavy arousal into her pelvis until she shut her eyes and arched her back. "It's been too long for you, Gaby. But, hell, am I glad, because you're going to be all the more for me."

"We shouldn't . . ." No, she would not say what she didn't feel or believe.

"Shouldn't we?" Bending, he slid his tongue across her lips, beneath them, past her teeth and deep into her mouth. Finesse was there but no restraint. He told her with every searching touch that he wanted her, and Gaby responded, yes, with a body wild, as it had never been before.

Jacques sipped and nipped and slanted his mouth over hers, rocking her head sharply, drawing her bottom lip between his teeth until she clung to him.

"We should definitely do all of this," he told her when he raised her head, in the instant before he bent to her breasts. "And I should definitely do this."

He supported the soft, aching weight, lightly pinched each nipple and took first one, then the other deep into his mouth. He drew firmly, suckled until Gaby filled her hands with his hair and opened her mouth in a silent scream.

"I want you," he said, rasping the demand. "Now."

His dark features sent white fire into Gaby's secret, hot places. Reason hovered at the edges of her mind. "We can't."

"We *can*." He gritted his teeth, kept his eyes on hers. "Come to me."

She shook her head. "We can't, Jacques." Surely he understood.

His hands were vices. They spanned her waist, but only for the moment before he tore open her jeans and skinned them to her ankles. Going to his knees, Jacques moaned. He cupped her bottom and kissed the shadowy triangle visible through red panties.

"Trust me, Gaby," he whispered, pulling

down the last barrier, heating her skin with his breath. "This is my game, remember?"

He moved smoothly then, stretching her out on the velvet grass he'd promised, dragging the jeans and panties from her feet, shedding his own pants and turning his back to her for the briefest moments.

"Jacques?"

"Oh, yes, quiet lady."

Then he dropped beside her, stroked her, kissed and caressed her. And all the time, while his shaft lay hot and heavy on her thigh, he murmured words that meant nothing except to him — and to her.

"God," he said at last, and very clearly. "I can't hold back, Gaby. Not any longer. Not this time."

She couldn't answer, but she ran her hands down until she could surround him. While her own heat mounted, Gaby closed the part of him that throbbed with need into her palms and pushed against the hair at its base until he cried out and rolled over her.

"Yes," she told him, parting her legs. "Yes."

"Open for me," he cried.

And she did.

Jacques cradled Gaby's hips and thrust into her with force that burned. Then there was the rhythm and the dance — and the endless joining that slammed them together as one.

"Now, Jacques."

"Soon." His thumb found the pulsing nub

that sent Gaby beyond reason. He ignored her flailing hands until she called his name over and over.

"That sounds so good," he told her. "My name never sounded that good."

Her body convulsed around him and he shouted his triumph.

12

"Champagne?"

"At nine in the morning?" Gaby turned from admiring the view and smiled at Jacques.

"I mixed it with orange juice."

"Mmm." Her smile widened. "Very nice."

"Why doesn't that sound like an endorsement of my mimosas?"

"I haven't tasted your mimosas."

He approached from the door that opened from his bedroom onto a terrace balanced between crystal-blue sky and a view of razorbacked hill and green valley devoid of any signs of civilization for as far as the eye could see.

Jacques slid a wooden tray onto a low, glass-topped table. "So," he said. "If it isn't my skill as a bartender that brings you pleasure, I'll just have to find out what does."

Gaby leaned against the terrace railings. Slow, moody music played through the sound system wired to every part of the house. "It may not be easy to get that information out of me. You could have to do some serious persuading." She crossed one bare foot over the other and cinched in the sash on the oversized, white terry robe she wore.

"How long will it take?" Jacques braced an arm each side of her on the railing. "I'm in a hurry to find out."

Gaby swayed to the music. With the backs of her fingers, she rubbed his jaw. "There are a lot of things left for us to find out about each other." Moisture from the shower gleamed in his still-wet hair and he smelled of soap. His robe matched Gaby's — except his fit him.

His gaze centered on her mouth and stayed there, until he tipped his head and bent to brush his lips across hers. "I never expected this." He closed his eyes and kissed her deeply.

Gaby stroked fingertips and palms down his neck and beneath the robe. He nudged her face up and she met his tongue hungrily.

When they'd finally left Jacques's valley the evening before, darkness had already begun to fall. The ride to La Place had been merely an intermission between acts of passion. In the hours they'd spent together, Gaby had learned what it was like to experience lovemaking with a man who knew as much about giving as taking. No millimeter of her body had escaped his attention.

Jacques drew back his head with the reluctance of a starving man letting go of a meal.

"No, I sure never expected this."

"What does that mean?" Gaby asked softly.

"Maybe I'm not sure." He frowned slightly. "But I would have laughed if someone had told me — even a few weeks ago — that I'd find a woman I could . . ." Looking away, he let the sentence trail off.

She would not press him to finish the thought.

"Gaby . . . Hell, I don't know. I think you've worn out my mind."

"Maybe you ought to get some sleep." She forced a laugh.

Jacques held up her hand and flattened the palm to his own. "I said my mind might be worn out. I didn't say anything about the rest of me."

Her hand looked like a child's against his, the fingers — long as they were — barely passing his second knuckle. "Those mimosas are getting warm," she said.

"Mmm." Lacing his fingers through Gaby's, Jacques pulled her into his arms. His body moved with the beat of a lone saxophone played with sensual languor — and his body moved Gaby's. With their locked hands trapped between them and Jacques holding her so close she almost heard the beat of his heart, Gaby felt the music, the rhythm, the beat through him.

They danced as only lovers dance.

Gaby looked up at him. His eyes were

closed, his lips parted.

But he wasn't smiling.

I never expected this . . .

She bit her lip. What hadn't he expected? To find a woman in little old Goldstrike who fitted him like a bespoke glove? To find what she knew he'd unearthed — what she'd found — a lover in tune with his wants, needs and desires before he knew them?

Or was there an even more outrageous reason why he'd stopped himself from finishing what he'd started to say?

Could she be feeling some of the same?

Gaby watched his eyelids clench and something close to pain pass over his face, features so boldly carved that most would assume him an arrogant man who had to know how startlingly handsome he was. And most would never discover the complex mix of tough and tender that lay behind that saturnine face.

Could they both be wondering if what they'd found might be more than a chemistry that made wonderful loving, wonderful sex? She turned her head away.

"What are you thinking?"

She jumped. "Nothing."

He bowed her backward until she laughed and grabbed for him. When he pulled her to him once more, the intensity in his eyes reminded Gaby of her nakedness beneath the robe — and of Jacques's sleek muscles. In the moonlight, coming to her on black satin sheets, on his own oversized bed, his body had gleamed. And in the aftermath of their climax, he'd allowed her to stretch out his arms and legs and smooth him from head to foot. And when it was time — he rolled to his stomach and the process had begun again.

Jacques's back was beautiful.

"Come on," he whispered above her head now, swinging them both in a circle. "Let me into those thoughts."

She pressed her lips to his naked chest where the robe parted. Sitting across his thighs in the silver light of slipping night, she'd brushed his back from shoulder to the twin dips at the base of his spine and over his hard buttocks.

And then she'd smiled . . . touched him somewhere else . . . and shrieked when he'd wrestled her beneath him . . .

"The devil made me do it!" she had yelled before his mouth closed out anything else she might have said.

Jacques tugged her ear gently. "Gaby?"

"Mmm?"

"The mimosas aren't all that's getting warm."

"Is the sun up?"

"It's been up."

She smiled into the hair on his chest. "Oh."

"Gaby."

Her smile broadened. "Mmm?"

"The sun isn't all that's up."

"Jacques!" Stepping away, she punched him playfully in the middle. "Shame on you. I thought you were a man of ideals. A man of *vision*."

Pretending agony, he gripped his stomach and tottered to fall into a chair. "I am a man of vision. I've already told you about my visions. You're not going to believe this, but I'm having another one right now."

As quickly as he'd laughed, the humor vanished from his face. "Come here." He patted his lap. "Right here."

Heat washed from Gaby's feet to her face. Deep inside she felt the burning ache she could so easily come to need.

"I want you, Gaby."

She couldn't have refused.

Jacques took her hands and brought her to stand between his legs. "First I want to look at you."

And he did look, for a long time, before hooking a hand behind her neck and pulling her face down to receive his slow, slow kiss. With the tip of his tongue, he outlined her mouth, then nipped her bottom lip gently and drew it between his teeth.

Still holding the kiss, he moved and guided her to sit astride his lap. "Why do we work so well together, Gaby?"

Startled, she raised her head. "I . . ." It wasn't such a strange question. "Lucky, I suppose. Maybe we should just enjoy it."

"You, my girl, are very forward."

She was not acting like herself. Tossing back her hair, she smiled into his eyes, navy-blue eyes — until the loving turned them deep, black-flecked indigo.

Dropping his head against the back of the chair, he raised his brows. "I think it's your turn."

Gaby understood.

She crossed her arms and worked the robe down her shoulders until only the fullness of her breasts stopped it from falling to her waist.

"Yeah," Jacques said, his voice deep and rough-edged. "Unwrap the package for me."

The morning air no longer felt cool. A pulse beat beneath her skin, gathering speed as she slid her hands beneath the robe to cup and lift her breasts, to offer them to Jacques with the arching of her back, the rocking of her hips.

Without holding her, he reached up and drew an erect nipple between his lips.

Gaby caught fire. "Jacques!"

"Yes, sweetheart, oh, yes."

"I can't take it."

In a single tug, the robe's sash hung loose and he smoothed her waist, her ribs and up to cover her breasts. "You can take it. We can both take it."

Gaby's legs trembled. "I want this thing off you," she told him, working open the single garment left between them. When she looked down at him, blood rushed to beat at her temples and tender parts of her body swelled.

"Are you sure you're ready for me?" He narrowed his eyes and ran his fingers through womanly hair. "I do believe you are."

"Should we go to bed?"

He shook his head. His grin was purely feral.

"You mean —" Breathing hard, she indicated the sky and the hills. "You mean, out here?"

"Uh-huh."

"In front of the world?"

"The thought appeals to me . . . again."

His fingers shifted and Gaby squeezed her eyes shut.

"D'you think you ought to make sure I'm ready?" Jacques said. Then he chuckled hoarsely. "You little puritan. You're blushing again. Do as you're told. Check everything out."

"I — can't think." Her pelvis jerked under his attention. She glanced down, over his beautifully defined chest, his flat stomach where black hair narrowed to a thin line, then flared again . . . and on to that which was so very ready.

The spasm he evoked with such ease broke

upon her. "Yes," she said through her teeth. "*Yes.*"

Jacques didn't have to help her. Gaby braced her hands on his chest, rose to her toes and sank, taking him inside her.

Black satin sheets forever!

Gaby luxuriated, stretched like a satisfied cat on the disarray that was Jacques's bed. The champagne and orange juice, her second, slid smoothly down her throat, leaving a tangy, bubbly taste on her tongue.

Pleading fear for their strength, Jacques had left to forage in the kitchen for emergency rations of food. And he'd absolutely refused to allow her to help him.

She could get really hooked on Jacques Ledan.

The telephone on the fax machine beside the bed rang. Seconds passed before Gaby looked disinterestedly at the single sheet of paper that rolled out.

The transmission ended.

Fax machines didn't belong in the bedroom. She stretched again and rolled to her stomach. The good news was that the presence of this machine probably meant Jacques was used to being here alone. That shouldn't matter, but it did.

Gaby looked down on the document that lay in the fax receiving tray.

To: Jacques
From: Bart
Subject: Napoleon Paradise

She turned her head away. Jacques's correspondence was none of her business.

Napoleon Paradise?

"Napoleon Paradise!" Gaby rose to her elbows. Everyone knew who that brilliant little eccentric was. Mr. Extravaganza himself, the recluse who lived on a private island in the south Pacific and created never-never land theme parks.

With a stomach that churned horribly, Gaby started reading the fax:

When he's ready, he's ready. If he says it's a go, the acreage starting at the old Odle place and covering the whole five-hundred-acre parcel will have to be clear-cut within a month. Then Napoleon will pay another visit. He says the leprechaun theme has "possibilities." Wants you to consider an adjoining hotel in conjunction with shuttle service to Tahoe. Thinks the gambling angle adds to sense of unreality.

Gaby dropped her forehead on her hands. *No!* There would be nothing left of Goldstrike by the time these maniacs finished.

She raised her head and continued reading:

187

He says he'll see you one week from yesterday, Saturday next. Be prepared for contract signing. He'll arrive in his own "amenities" — whatever that means, and will expect you to receive him at nine in the evening.

This guy is a fruitcake. Only conducts business between nine at night and four in the morning.

Almost forgot. Wear a tux! Napoleon says he is always "an event" worth dressing for.

PS. Acknowledge this. Where the hell are you?

Gaby heard approaching footsteps in the hall and pressed her face into the pillow. *Be prepared for contract signing?* And just like that a decision would be made that would change Goldstrike forever. Her mind raced in circles. What had passed between her and Jacques meant something, didn't it? Surely he'd be more willing to listen to her now.

Perhaps he'd even change his mind completely. . . .

The door opened to Jacques's vocal attempt at "Music of the Night" from *Phantom of the Opera.*

He *had* to change his mind. She would make him — somehow.

"Gaby, love? Hungry?"

She didn't move. Whatever happened, she

must not let him know she'd seen the fax.

"Sleepyhead," he murmured.

Sounds of dishes clinking followed. Then the bed sank under his weight and he sat beside her.

Gaby squeezed her eyes more tightly shut. He'd had this house a long time. Regardless of what Jacques intended to do in the area, he wouldn't suddenly stop coming here when the project was finished . . . would he?

Her stomach turned again. Was that it? Had the motivation behind her opposition of the project changed? Did she fear the loss of Jacques more than the loss of Goldstrike?

The crackle of paper almost stopped her heart. She held her breath.

"Ass," she heard him mutter at last. Then the paper rustled again and he rested a hand between her shoulders. Very lightly Jacques caressed the line of her spine all the way to the point where the satin sheet barely covered her bottom. That's where he kissed her.

The air rushed from her lungs, but she held still.

Spreading his fingers, he spanned her waist and began to skim upward over her ribs — to the place where her breasts rested. Jacques feathered over that soft flesh until Gaby could be still no longer. She attempted to twist toward him. Jacques's response was to slip his hands beneath her breasts and lean to kiss the back of her neck.

"You look good here," he said, nuzzling aside her hair. "Right."

Gaby felt tears spring into her eyes. He could not know how certain innocent little phrases played with the heart.

"Out in the hills — when I found you yesterday — you said I already knew you. What did you mean by that?"

"Exactly what I said."

Carefully, he turned her to her back. "I guess I'm missing something. I didn't know who you were until someone told me."

"Yes you did." She met his eyes steadily. "I meant that I am what you see. I'm not what I do or where I've been or with whom."

Jacques lifted her hands to his mouth, kissed each knuckle with absorption and stretched her arms above her head. "Don't you think where we've been and who we've been there with affects us as people?"

"They may cause a few wrinkles in the wrappings. Inside we're still the same."

The way he stroked the sensitive inner sides of her arms made Gaby flinch and breathe harder. Jacques, wearing sweatpants and nothing else, studied her face, her body. He suddenly smiled and dropped a kiss on her belly. "You're a deep woman, Gaby McGregor."

Yet again his lips and fingers began to work their magic. She willed herself not to react.

Abruptly he released her arms and swept her up into his embrace. "Would you like to take me for what I am, Gaby? And what I'm not?"

The tension in his voice squeezed her heart. "Yes," she said simply, nestling — so naturally — into the warmth of his big body.

"I'm glad. That would be a first."

"People like you identify with things, Jacques. I don't. I don't want to know Jacques Ledan, multi-millionaire candy king. It's what's inside that counts."

He became absolutely still. "Why do I almost believe you?"

She bit back the anger that surged. "Because it's true. Not everyone is in love with wealth and everything that comes with it." This wasn't the time to explain that she could have lived — could still live — the so-called good life. "I'd like you just as much if you were . . . a farmer or a man struggling with some little business. You'd still be you."

"Would I?" He put her gently from him, pulled the pillows up behind her head. "That's a unique thought. I may have to work it through. I brought coffee and sandwiches."

Settling herself, but unable to relax, Gaby tucked the top sheet up to her armpits. "Jacques." There might never be a better time. "Could we talk about Goldstrike?"

He paused in the act of pouring coffee. "If you like. Cream and sugar?"

"No, thanks. Some of what you propose may have very positive results."

"I'm glad you approve."

His sarcasm stung. "You said you would discuss this."

"And I am." He gave her a mug, put a plate of sandwiches on the bed and sat in a chair.

With her eyes on the coffee in her mug, Gaby took several slow sips. "Would you be prepared to consider some compromises?"

He stared at her. "I always listen to reasonable people's opinions."

Unfortunately she hadn't prepared for this opportunity. Whatever argument she came up with would be grabbed from the air. "My idea is that you meet with a delegation of residents to talk over what is or isn't acceptable." She almost winced at the dictatorial note in her own voice.

After several seconds he slipped lower in the chair and stretched out his legs. "I won't be *told* what to do, Gaby. I'm putting a lot of money into this. And my motives are good, I assure you. The best. Sometimes people are too emotional to see what's advantageous for them."

"But you never are?" She sat up and pushed her mug onto the bedside table. "I think you're arrogant, Jacques. You decide what other people want and need then set about persuading them you're right."

"Calm down."

"Calm . . ." She seethed. "Would you mind leaving the room. I'd like to get dressed."

"Women!" He looked at the ceiling.

Gaby could barely contain herself. "I'll let that pass. Please do as I ask. I've got to get Vi back."

"You called and said you'd be keeping her until this evening."

"I've changed my mind."

He got to his feet, picked up her mug and pressed it back into her hands. "When does Mae get back?"

"Late tonight."

"Char Brown is a sort of substitute grand-mother, isn't she?"

Gaby glared at him. "Yes."

"Good."

Furious that he could be so calm, she continued drinking her coffee.

"Aren't you going to ask me why it's good?"

She shook her head.

"Because we're going to need plenty of op-portunities to be together."

"You . . . You are so pig-headed."

"Are you saying you don't want to make love on the grass again and against a tree and on a terrace and in my bed . . . and on a horse?"

Gaby sputtered and coughed. "We *didn't* make love on a horse."

"Exactly. We've got something to look forward to."

Despite her ire, Gaby smiled into her cup. "What an impossible man."

"What a maddening little hatter," Jacques said quietly. "And I really do like you for exactly what you are. If you want me to speak with some of the residents, I'll be happy to do that."

She turned a brilliant grin on him. "You will? Oh, thank you, Jacques. I know how much it will mean to them to discover you really care about their opinions."

"I *do* care about their opinions. I always have. I care about *them.* That's why I started all this in the first place."

The temptation was to say that he'd long ago stopped putting the needs and wants of the community first. "I'll arrange a meeting."

"Fine. We'll get to it when we can."

Gaby's eyes went to the pocket of his sweats where the folded fax was visible. "This is asking a lot. But could you hold off on starting anything major until after we've had the talk?"

His eyes moved from hers. "We can try."

"You won't regret it, Jacques." Thinking rapidly, she passed her tongue over dry lips.

"Saturday nights are pretty quiet around here. People are usually available. I'll set something up for next Saturday evening, if that's okay with you?"

"Saturday?" He started to nod, then narrowed his eyes and rested a hand on his pocket. "No. Not Saturday."

She swallowed. "That's too bad. Got to go back to civilization and see to business?"

"Yes . . . no." Jacques cracked a tight smile. "I just remembered that's the night I promised my folks I'd talk to them. They live in the south of France and they're always so busy I have to make an appointment to get on their schedule."

"Will talking to them take all night?" Bit by bit she felt the intimacy they'd built dissolve. "We could make it later. Say nine?"

"I can't be sure we'll be through."

"Ten."

"We might not be finished." He stood. "Look, why don't we work this out later. For the following Saturday, perhaps?"

By which time the command performance with Napoleon Paradise would have taken place and, quite possibly, the kind of contract signed that would be almost impossible to scuttle.

"D'you think that would work out for your people?"

Her people. Not the people he was so concerned about that he was dragging them into his "progress" whether they liked it or not.

"Gaby?"

She looked into his eyes and read anxiety there. "That'll probably be fine." Did he think she couldn't figure out that they'd found something pretty rare, even if it was only physical — at least on his side — and that he didn't want to jeopardize that? "Yes. I'll see what I can do."

"Great!" He set down his mug and took hers away.

"Mmm. Great," Gaby agreed.

And his arms and body, enfolding her once more, felt wonderful. Damn it, but she wanted him, would continue to want him and with a whole lot more than that part of her that caught fire when he touched her — looked at her, even.

Jacques pressed her back on the bed and settled his length beside her.

Gaby saw his eyes close. Holding him felt natural, peaceful. She wanted him and he wanted her . . . and those were the facts she'd have to use for another purpose, at least once.

Maddening hatter? He didn't know how maddening yet.

Jacques Ledan wouldn't be meeting with Napoleon Paradise next Saturday evening.

13

"Talk to him, Bart."

"I have, sweetheart. You can see how far it's gotten me."

Rita slung her purse on top of Jacques's desk. "Try again. Pl-ea-se."

"You try," Bart said from the depths of the canvas director chair — complete with his name on the back — that he'd produced the previous week. "I've got too much on my mind with Napoleon coming."

"If Jacques can't get his head together, Napoleon might as well *not* come."

"Shut — Be quiet," Jacques said from his post overlooking Gaby's skylight. "And give me the respect of not talking as if I weren't present."

"Thank God," Rita said in breathy tones. "He's returned to us. Jacques, we've got to go over everything before Napoleon Paradise descends — or skates in, or however he intends to arrive."

"And we will go over everything," Jacques told her, barely containing his irritation. "I don't enjoy working with panicky people.

You're panicking, Rita. *Don't.*"

"Hey." Bart shoved himself to his feet and draped an arm around Rita's shoulders. "Rita's been working very hard, Jacques, for a long time. We both have. But this project hasn't been easy on her. She's not a country girl."

Interest sparked in Jacques. Bart was becoming quite the White Knight considering he and Rita were always fighting.

"I think you take Rita entirely too much for granted."

"Thank you," Rita said, bestowing a tremblingly grateful smile on Bart. "But it's you he really underestimates."

Jacques saw what he'd waited all day to see: Gaby leaving the courtyard on her bicycle.

"No, sweetheart," Bart said to Rita. "You're very generous, but —"

"But I underestimate you both. Why don't the two of you stick around here and compare notes. I've got some very important business to attend to. When it's done, I'll be back." Jacques headed for the stairs. "Make yourselves at home. Anything you want you'll find in the kitchen. If you get tired . . . well, there's a bed. Please feel free to take a nap."

At his last backward glance he saw them continuing to gaze at each other, apparently oblivious either to him or his remarks.

This time he would judge everything exactly right, do everything perfectly. The moment had come to be up front with Gaby — as honest as he could be. He ought to be able to deal with small difficulties without lying.

At the side of the building, perched on ridiculously oversized wheels, stood a new, glossy red van, belonging to Ozzie Odle, the truculent son of the family whose farm Jacques had bought. Ozzie had no interest in farming and had seemed grateful to be relieved of the potential burden of trying to carry on for his father one day. With the money that had apparently been his portion of what Jacques had paid for the farm, Ozzie had started what he called a "convenience" business. This seemed to involve sitting around all day drinking beer whilst, with the aid of his silver-striped van, being prepared to accommodate the needs of others.

"Here we go, Ozzie," Jacques called.

The gangly young man levered himself from a perch on an upturned crate, burped and crushed his beer can. "I was thinking, Mr. Ledan," he said, ambling toward Jacques, a puckish frown on his long face. "How would it be if I had GFTG painted on the doors of the van?"

Jacques paused. "Why would you do that?"

Ozzie shrugged inside a shrunken T-shirt that rode up over a pot belly. "Seems t'me there'll be plenty of fetchin' and carryin' you'll be needin' around here. Might as well advertise while I'm about it."

Jacques hid a grin. "We'll see, Ozzie." The more good will he could engender the better. "That might work. Right now we need to get to that little matter we discussed earlier. I want you to do what we planned. Follow me. Don't get too close until I'm inside the house."

He jogged to the Jeep and set off. He had to stop once to remind Ozzie to fall back. After that the other vehicle remained at an acceptable distance.

When he drove up to Gaby's house he checked his watch. Three. Should be enough time before the child arrived.

Gaby took a long time to open the door.

He bent to kiss her.

She stepped back, left the door open and walked away through the house.

With raised brows, Jacques followed. "Hello, Gaby. I've missed you. How are you? Have you had a nice day? Did work go well?"

She went into a small sitting room. Through French windows he could see a vegetable garden.

Jacques tried again. "Now you're supposed to be nice to me."

"Am I?"

"Okay, I give up. What did I do wrong?"

He wished he didn't feel so damned guilty. At least he could be certain she didn't know he'd lied through his teeth to her, so why feel bad?

Gaby sighed. "You didn't do anything. I'm a very unpredictable person, is all. You just don't know me well enough to recognize one of my mood swings."

"I know you *very* well." Approaching, he held out his arms.

She dodged away and sat in an overstuffed chintz chair. "No you don't. If you did, you wouldn't like me."

Postcoital remorse? "Probably not. I'll take my chances." From his pocket he pulled a red velvet bag. "Here. You undoubtedly won't like it. Take it, anyway."

Gaby watched him drop it into her lap, and he took pleasure in the spark of anticipation she wasn't quick enough to hide.

"Open it."

"What is it?"

"*Gaby.*"

Scowling afresh, she loosened the drawstring that closed the top and removed the bag's contents.

"It's nothing," Jacques said. He strolled to a bookcase and ran a forefinger along titles. A hodgepodge of everything including ten-year-old tax preparation tables. "Give it to Mae to dress up in."

"Jacques." She whispered his name with

satisfactory awe and he smiled.

"How would you describe your taste in literature?"

"Where on earth did you get this? Bananas and cherries and strawberries . . ."

"And bunches of grapes. I called a friend in LA last night. He rounded the necklace up and had it brought in by chopper early this morning." He eased out a leatherbound copy of Homer's *Iliad* and turned to Gaby. "This is pretty heavy stuff for someone with . . . eclectic taste? You've kept it in great condition."

Squinting at the book, Gaby pushed her lips out in a pout, then her expression cleared. "I've never opened it, that's why it's in great condition. Jacques, stop behaving as if a beautiful gold necklace studded with what appear to be emeralds, sapphires and rubies — and designed to echo my fruit theme for the year — were nothing."

"They are emeralds, sapphires and rubies. The sapphires and rubies are incidental. The emeralds are a stone you should wear all the time. They are exactly the color of your eyes."

She made an unintelligible noise.

"Don't mumble. May I put it on you? It'll look great with the green silk dress."

"I can't take it."

He'd anticipated this. "No, I didn't think

so. Ah, well. How do you think emeralds look on blonds?"

"Blonds?"

"It was modified to my specification. In a few hours. It isn't on approval so I can't send it back."

"Oh."

He averted his eyes, but not before he saw her frown. "Don't worry, Gaby. Rita tells me Camilla Roberts is still in town. I suppose —"

"Put it on me — just so we can see what it looks like."

"Of course."

Gaby turned her back to him and he arranged the necklace, a heavy collar formed of links shaped like fruits and discreetly studded with gems, about her throat.

He rested his hands on her shoulders.

She remained where she was, head bent forward.

"I don't think this would look at all good on a blond," Jacques said. Just touching her made his body tighten. "It needs black silk, like your hair, to show it off."

"Does it?"

"Uh-huh." There was no question of not kissing that soft, white skin on the side of her neck, and he did so now. "And my sheets would complete the picture."

"Jacques," she said, very low, but there was little reproach in her voice. "You shouldn't have done this."

"Yes I should." He spun her around. "You told me about the fruit theme yesterday — in the madrone — and I wished I had some beautiful symbol of your enthusiasm to lay on your skin right then."

Her eyes were luminous. "I haven't said I'll keep it."

"But you will."

"I'll think about it. In the meantime, thank you, Jacques. Thank you so much for making me feel special. It's been a long time since . . . Well, thank you."

Shaking her gently, he lifted her chin with a knuckle. "If it's been a long time since a man gave you beautiful things it's because you haven't let anyone get close to you. I'm glad you haven't. But if you wanted a line of males begging you to receive their favors you'd only have to crook a little finger, my love." Perhaps he only imagined that she looked troubled but he experienced an unwelcome twinge of apprehension.

She fingered the gold collar. "I'm really not sure I should accept this."

Illumination dawned. "Are you afraid people around here will think you're selling out on them?"

Her heightened color gave him his answer. "Not really."

Jacques made a decision. "Will you come to LA with me the weekend after next?"

"LA?"

"Yes. You know — that city you don't really like too much anymore."

"I know what you mean by LA."

"Will you come?" The surprise on her face was no act. He'd have to talk fast if he hoped to persuade her. "We'd fly, of course. Mae could come along and visit her father while you're with me."

She looked increasingly doubtful. "I don't think that's such a great idea."

"Why not?"

"Well . . . I wouldn't want Michael to think —" She bit her lip.

"You've been divorced for seven years, for crying out loud. Does he live like a monk?"

"I doubt it."

"That's that angle covered, then." The thought that Gaby hadn't been involved with a man since her husband brought enormous pleasure. "Has Mae been in a chopper before?"

"A helicopter?" Gaby shook her head. "Neither have I."

"You'll both love it. And she'll be able to tell all the kids in school about it."

"I really don't know," Gaby said. "I'll have to think about it."

At the sound of the front door opening and slamming shut again, Jacques had to stifle a groan. Within seconds Mae McGregor tore into the room, dropping miscellaneous articles on the way. "Hi, Mom. I got a hundred on my spelling quiz. Mrs. Delany says I should enter the spelling bee in the spring. Mary-Alice Healy is a pain. She's mad because she didn't get a hundred, and —" Mae stopped. "You're here again," she said to Jacques.

"I certainly am. I came to see you and your mother. How was your visit to your dad's?"

"Great. He and his friend took me to this really neat place where only grown-ups go. They sit on stools drinking weird-colored stuff and looking around. Dad laughs about it. He says they're all looking to see who's looking at them."

"Sounds like a lot of fun." To Jacques it sounded anything but fun. "Is his friend nice?"

Mae considered. "She's okay for a bimbo."

"*What?*" Gaby said.

"Dad says Toby's okay for a bimbo but he wouldn't want to make a habit of her. She makes great ice cubes, though."

Jacques didn't dare look at Gaby.

"She's got these shaped trays she keeps in Daddy's freezer for when she comes over. Mouths and hearts and elephants, teddy bears. Toby likes them in her pop and she lets me have some."

"It was nice of you to come over, Jacques," Gaby said. Her eyes had turned a dark, glittery green. "We'll talk again soon."

If he wasn't careful, he wasn't going to

make all the points he'd intended to make today. "We sure will. Wait here a minute. There's something I want to do before I leave."

Gaby followed him into the hall, her hands clasped in front of her.

Breaking the silence, Jacques said, "Stay right where you are." At the door, he hesitated. "You will think about LA? About coming with me?"

A mutinous frown brought her fine brows together. "If I go, Mae won't be with me. She won't be visiting Michael again until I'm sure the situation's suitable."

"You're so right. It'll be the perfect opportunity to check that out. Wait there, okay?"

"Okay."

Jacques opened the door, poked his head out and gestured extravagantly.

"Are you all right?" Gaby asked from behind.

"Great!" He faced her again. "Never better."

"Good." Gaby rocked from her heels to her toes and back. "Was there something else you wanted to say?"

"The necklace looks wonderful on you."

"I probably shouldn't keep it."

"*Don't* . . . Please don't start that again. You've already accepted it and that gives me great pleasure."

"It's not right for me to take gifts from you."

He glanced out the door again. "I forced it on you. Leave it at that."

"Jacques, you're behaving very strangely."

"I know. I mean, no I'm not." He bent to smile at Mae, who had come to stand beside her mother. "Mae, close your eyes."

When she'd done so, he threw open the door and waved Ozzie Odle into the entrance hall.

"Oh, Jacques," Gaby moaned. "Get that out of here!"

"Open your eyes, Mae. I brought you a present."

The child promptly obeyed. For an instant she was speechless. Then, crooning and clapping her hands, she dropped to her knees. "Oh, he's *beautiful*. Wait till I show him to Mary-Alice."

Gaby stabbed a finger in Jacques's direction and moved her lips silently. Finally, with obvious effort, she said, "A pig?"

Hacienda Heaven wasn't Gaby's favorite watering hole, but today was Tuesday. On Tuesdays she and Char came to Barney's for burners because Char loved them.

"I think he's a doll," Char said, sucking the last of a margarita noisily through her straw. "He obviously wants to make you happy."

"By dumping a pig on me?" Gaby said morosely.

"A piglet," Char corrected. "And he even

supplied a little house for it."

"A sty, not a house. Pigs live in sties."

"Snap him up while you've got the chance is what I say. If you don't, someone else will. The man's obviously ripe for romance."

And so was Gaby. "He is special," she admitted reluctantly.

"Way to go!" Char batted Gaby's arm. The weekly margarita invariably loosened her inhibitions even more than usual. "Seven years as a frustrated female are enough."

"Who says I've been frustrated?"

Char ignored the question. "Go to LA with him. What have you got to lose?"

She'd already lost her heart. "Nothing."

"And don't make such a big deal out of the Toby thing. Michael wouldn't do anything to hurt Mae and you know it. He adores that child."

"He didn't want her."

"He does now. Quit changing the subject. Go to LA with Jacques. You're already in love with him."

Gaby took away Char's straw. "You don't know that. Don't say it again."

"Because it's true?" Char held up a hand. "All right. I won't say it again."

It was true. Perhaps she should come clean with Jacques about having seen the fax and ask him to reconsider seeing Napoleon Paradise. She didn't know for certain he'd been dishonest with her on Sunday. Not completely. He probably did have to speak to his parents next Saturday and he simply hadn't thought to mention Napoleon as well.

"Will you go?" Char wheeled.

"Maybe."

"It's the right thing to do."

"You're probably right."

Barney, polishing the bar to stay within hearing distance, put down his cloth and grinned. "Well, as I live and breathe, if it isn't Sophie Byler."

"Sophie?" Gaby and Char said in unison, turning to see their friend, her back very straight, marching toward them.

"Good day to you, Barney." After placing her purse precisely on the bar, she hitched herself onto a stool like a woman who had never sat on such a contraption before — which she probably never had. Sophie disapproved — often loudly — of bars, of Barney and of the Hacienda Heaven. "Leprechaun auditions," she said clearly.

Gaby looked at Char.

"Leprechaun auditions," Sophie repeated.

"It's all right, Sophie," Gaby said kindly. "Something's upset you. Tell us about it."

Sophie clenched and unclenched her hands in her lap. "It'll be like the bumper cars at a fair, only reversed."

Char left her stool and went to put an arm around Sophie's shoulders. "Would you like some water?"

"No! He's holding auditions for leprechauns for his horrible park. Don't you understand?" Sophie began to shake.

"Sophie —" Bewildered, Gaby shook her head.

"There's going to be a bar for testing how tall the applicants are," Sophie continued, her eyes glassy. "Only instead of having to be taller than the bar — like it is when you want to ride on the bumper cars — you'll have to be shorter if you want to be hired as one of Ledan's leprechauns."

"I see," Gaby said slowly. He'd said he was willing to discuss his plans before rushing ahead. "When exactly are these *auditions?*"

"Barney." Sophie opened her purse. "I'll take a pail of margaritas, please."

"That's a bucket," Barney corrected.

"You don't drink," Char told Sophie.

"*When?*" Gaby persisted. Her stomach cramped. If she'd already eaten a burner there'd be reason to suspect food poisoning.

"Weekend after next," Sophie announced. "Saturday and Sunday at the old fire station."

"Oh, dear," Char said. "That's the weekend Gaby's going —"

Gaby brought a small fist down on the bar. "I'm *not* going to LA. Sneaky rat. All he wants is to stop me from being around to interfere with his plans. Barney!"

"Yes, Gaby."

"We'll have that bucket of margaritas."

14

"He'll lie through his teeth," Gaby said, filing into the Women's Auxiliary Hall behind Char.

"At least he changed his mind about making time to talk with all of us tonight," Char said. "Give the man a chance."

Give him a chance? "What do you think I've been doing?"

Char raised a single eyebrow at Gaby and said nothing.

Gaby felt herself turn pink. She hadn't actually *said* she and Jacques were lovers, but Char's sharp-eyed glance suggested she'd arrived at that conclusion. "Promise me you'll take good care of Mae tonight," Gaby whispered urgently.

"As if I'd do anything else." Char didn't deign to look at Gaby again. "I've been loving her since she was a baby. Why would that change just because her mother's turned into a pig-headed idiot?"

"*Don't* mention pigs to me."

"Hush. He's coming."

Jacques was indeed coming to the gathering

he'd called for seven o'clock on the very Saturday evening when he intended to give Goldstrike's history to a carnival maker.

Striding through the double doors of the creaking, white clapboard building, he smiled from side to side and waved like a confident young politician . . . or a television evangelist.

A television evangelist in a *tuxedo*.

Gaby's blood began to simmer. "*Now* do you believe what I told you?" She crossed her arms and shrank against the back wall. "Look what he's wearing."

Char's brow puckered. "He could have decided this was an occasion for formal dress."

"A chat with people he considers the insignificant local yokels of Goldstrike? Oh, give me a break!"

Jacques leaped up the steps to the platform and smiled his marvelous smile in all directions as if waiting for applause to cease.

Silence had fallen upon the previously grumbling audience.

"Good evening to you all," Jacques said, bracing his feet apart and managing to make his deep, clear voice carry throughout the hall. "I really appreciate your cooperation. You didn't get much notice about tonight's meeting, and this is a great turnout."

"He makes it sound as if all he did was post a flyer on a tree," Gaby whispered. "Hand-delivered invitations complete with the promise of complementary Ledan chocolates might just have swayed one or two into appearing."

"He was being gracious. And he's here to make you happy. If you hadn't given him the cold shoulder all week he probably wouldn't have bothered." Char sighed. "He's *so* good-looking."

Char was another Jacques Ledan conquest. Gaby looked over the women present and decided they all appeared dazed by Mr. Wonderful.

"I'm sure you all have other things to do on a Saturday night, so I'll keep this brief," Jacques said.

"Because *he* has other things to do," Gaby intoned. "Only he's not going to get to do them."

Char glanced at her. "I hope you know what you're doing."

"What would you say to a new school right here in Goldstrike?" Jacques's voice rang out.

A rumble of conversation broke out among the assembly.

"Would having your children go to school in their community again please you?"

Scattered shouts of Yes rose.

"We can do that, my friends. You and I as a team can bring our children back where they belong. With the healthy, and very acceptable, rise in population my expansion plans will bring, there'll be enough young people in Goldstrike to warrant providing for their education in the town where they live. And — when they graduate and, we hope, go on to college — they'll leave with enough enthusiasm for their hometown to want to *come back!*

"I say, let's get rid of busing for good. Let's take back the right, and the opportunity, to have a real impact on the formative years of our greatest resource — our young people!"

"Yes!" The response was deafening.

Jacques grinned endearingly. He strolled back and forth on the stage like a pleased, exceptionally handsome and wholesome movie star who had proven that his vaguely devilish face and lean, commanding body, were merely a disguise.

A big man in the center of the crowd rose to his feet.

"That's one of Sis's brothers," Char said. "I didn't think they spoke."

The following silence lasted so long, Gaby began to believe the man must be mute.

He coughed, hitched at baggy blue overalls and coughed. "What's it all going to cost us, then? That's what we want to know. Don't get nothin' for nothin' in our book. Our Sis says you're plannin' to change everythin' around here. We wouldn't hold with that. No sir." Abruptly he sat down again.

Jacques leveled a long finger on the man.

"I'm very glad you said that. Very glad. If I don't hear these silly rumors, I can't put your worries to bed. And that's where they belong, folks. I want you to trust me. I've been coming to Goldstrike since I was a baby. My grandfather built a little house — not much more than a cabin — where La Place stands now. My father enlarged the building and I've added on a room or two."

"It's the size of a castle," Gaby mumbled.

"My family and I have a stake in this area and that's why I'm setting out to make a new future for all of us. It would take too long to explain everything we intend to do, but I've got a compromise."

"A compromise that'll get him to a more important meeting on time," Gaby said.

"Shh." Char pressed a finger to her lips.

"Within a month there'll be a detailed mock-up of the entire project available for viewing."

Gaby shifted. "He makes it sound like a body."

"As soon as the location's been fixed, I'll make sure every one of you is informed. I'll be personally responsible for conducting lectures with full explanations of each phase."

"Mae's playing out front," Gaby said. "I'd better get started."

"I really wish you wouldn't."

"He's got to be stopped."

A smattering of applause gusted through

the room, and Gaby glanced at Jacques once more. He looked directly at her and smiled. "Please believe me when I say that what happens here is important to me personally." His mouth became serious, but he continued to hold Gaby's gaze. "In fact, it's very probable that you can expect me to be spending more and more time in Goldstrike."

She made herself look away.

"I've got to leave you," Jacques announced. "But first I'm going to show you just one reason why I'm determined to change the future for all of us. Come here, Mae."

Gaby froze.

Through the doors came Mae. Jacques jumped down from the platform and strode to meet the child. He gave her ponytail a playful tug and took her small hand in his. Side by side they walked to the front of the hall and Jacques lifted Mae to stand before the townspeople.

"That's it," Gaby said through barely parted lips. "Now he's really going to find out who can play dirty."

From the floor, Jacques indicated Gaby's adorable daughter. "Mae McGregor is a friend of mine. And she's just one of many reasons why we've got to band together as a team and make a future worth having."

With that he bent to retrieve the companion Mae had brought with her. "We're going to make sure this is always a down home place where children can grow up enjoying the special things city kids only dream about." He set Mae's new piglet on the platform. "Meet Shortcake. He belongs to Mae. My parting words to you are — A pig for every kid. Thank you for coming."

"You're going to wish *you* hadn't come, Jacques," Gaby said as she dashed from the hall.

He never remembered holding a child's hand before. An alien, poignant sensation surprised him. Mae was an intelligent little girl, full of fun, but with a serious side, too. Yeah, he might be able to enjoy her . . . only because she was Gaby's though, of course.

Jacques drove the Jeep away from the Women's Auxiliary Hall. As he'd walked down the aisle to leave, the tentative smiles and nods from a number of people had pleased him.

Insisting on attending the meeting alone had been a master stroke. He would enjoy telling Bart and Rita how right he'd been to think people would see him as more accessible without an entourage. Too bad he'd had no choice but to go in the tux. Bart had called on the car phone to say Napoleon Paradise was canceling until further notice, but by then Jacques was already driving into

Goldstrike and it had been too late to go back and change.

Slipping a finger beneath his starched collar, he twisted his neck uncomfortably. Black tie was fine in its place but not in Goldstrike.

On the edge of town he drew to the side of the road, trying to make up his mind which way to go. Straight ahead and home, or to the right and Gaby's house.

When he'd left the hall, Char Brown had been the one to collect Mae. Gaby was nowhere to be seen, and he hadn't liked to ask Char where she was in front of the child.

Gaby hadn't said more than two or three short sentences to him all week.

But maybe she'd be looser now he'd given the local people the hearing she'd so badly wanted.

The minute he'd made eye contact with her, she'd walked out.

Damn. He gunned the engine and pointed the Jeep's nose straight ahead. Let her be the one to make the next move. He'd never had to run after a woman and he didn't intend to start now.

The evening was gray. A fine rain misted the windshield. Jacques settled his elbow on the window ledge and drove the road instinctively. Why hadn't he gotten involved in the town before?

No reason to, he guessed. That and the

fact that he used to feel completely involved with Ledan's. But no man with imagination could be expected never to crave new ventures, ventures conceived and executed by himself.

Ahead, something moved.

Jacques leaned forward and peered. The road rose and fell gently at this point and the failing light flattened everything.

A figure knelt on the shoulder beside a pile of something he couldn't make out.

As he drew closer, Jacques slowed down. Then the person stood up.

"Gaby?" It was Gaby. She waved. The pile consisted of her bicycle, resting on its side with one wheel unattached.

Jacques pulled over and got out. Immediately the rain, heavier now, buffeted him. "What are you *doing*, woman?" He strode to stand over the cycle.

"Trying to fix this." Gaby sounded doleful as she pointed to the dismembered machine.

"Out here?" He looked in all directions. "Why are you riding out here?"

"I like to," she said, without inflection.

A thought struck him. She'd ridden out here *hoping* to see him. Why else? "It is pretty scenery, isn't it?" His heart warmed. He'd wanted her to make a move. This was it. But he mustn't spook her by letting her know he'd guessed.

"I don't suppose you know anything about

bicycles." The resigned way she spoke suggested she doubted he'd ever done anything practical in his life.

"Let me take a look." This wasn't the time to tell her he came from very sensible stock who believed in self-sufficiency.

Crouching, he grasped the bike's front fork and pulled the loose wheel into place. "The release couldn't have been secure. This won't take a minute." Then he'd pack her — and the bike — into the Jeep and take them home. To his home.

"Something rolled away," Gaby said. "Over there. Behind you."

Jacques swiveled in the direction she pointed. Gaby, stumbling into him, was a blur he saw the moment before she knocked him to his back on dirt that was rapidly turning muddy.

"I'm sorry," Gaby wailed. "Oh, dear."

Somehow they became jumbled together on the ground. With legs flailing, she clutched his shirt with both hands as if trying to save herself from impact.

"We've already fallen," Jacques said, as evenly as he could. All he could do was hold on while she squirmed all over him. "Gaby, it's over. We can get up again now."

"Oh, dear. Oh, dear!"

"Gaby, you're strangling me."

"Oh —" Her eyes widened and she grew still. "Oh. I'm sorry."

"It's okay. Accidents happen."

The white dress she wore was wet — and getting wetter. "I don't know what happened. I'm *so* sorry. With her body stretched on top of him, her eyes were very close — and very green. "You must think I'm a total klutz."

Jacques tried for a patient smile. "Not a bit of it, sweetheart. But it might be nice to get up."

"Get up? Oh, of course." Still holding the lapels of his jacket, she crawled off and knelt beside him. "Let me help you."

"We'll throw the bike in the Jeep and get out of this rain," he told her. "We're both getting soaked."

"Look at your shirt, Jacques. It's a mess."

He did look, and wince. Thank God he wasn't trying to make the meeting with Napoleon.

Gaby smoothed the tux — with muddy hands — and tutted.

There were times when the behavior of women completely confounded him. He got up and pulled Gaby to her feet. "In the Jeep. I'll deal with the bike."

"It's closer to my house than yours."

Jacques opened the door. "I don't think so."

"I do." Gaby climbed into the Jeep. "In fact, I know it is. And I know you're in a hurry to get to . . . to get somewhere important."

He tried to close the door but she held it open. "Gaby, relax. Don't give this another thought. We'll go to my place and get warm." He looked at his watch, calculating whether or not his cook would have left and decided she undoubtedly had.

"What time is it?"

"Eight-fifteen," he told her.

"That late? You must be beside yourself with me. Please, Jacques. Forget the bike. I'll find a way to pick it up later."

He leaned closer to examine her face, particularly her forehead. There was no sign of a bump or cut. "You're shaken up." Gently removing her hand from the window rim, he shut her in. "Close your eyes and rest." From the way she was acting, a complete head check might be a good idea.

Quickly he manhandled the bike behind his seat and hopped in beside Gaby.

"Your clothes are a mess," she said.

"They sure are." Thanks to her efforts. "So are yours. We'll get to La Place. You can take a nice, long, hot bath while I do what I have to." The call to his parents would still need to be made, and he might as well get it out of the way early.

"My house really is closer." Gaby clamped a hand on the steering wheel. "It is."

"I think mine's closer." And there was no danger of being interrupted.

"You're wrong. Mine is. I've measured."

He spread his fingers on his thighs. "Measured?"

"I mean . . . Not exactly *measured*. But I've spent so much time out here I just *know*."

"I see."

"I knew you would."

"You really don't want to come to my house, do you?"

"No — I mean, *yes,* yes, of course I do. It's just that with you being in such a hurry and needing to arrive where you're going in a tux, I'm sure I can fix you up quickly at my house and —" she paused for breath "— and then you can be on your way and not make anyone upset or miss anything you've got to do."

The poor little thing felt guilty! Jacques smiled and said soothingly, "All right. Your house it'll be." He was going to have to work harder on helping her build self-esteem. No doubt that creep Michael Copeland was the kind of man who berated women for the smallest mistake.

After backing up, Jacques swung the Jeep around and headed back the way he'd come. At the junction he turned left and floored the accelerator. Gaby was definitely soaked and the anxiety on her face troubled him. He didn't know all the pressures she was under. A woman at peace with herself and the world didn't ride around the wide open spaces in bad weather — on a bicycle — even in hopes of seeing a man who interested her.

"Will Char and Mae be there?"

"No!"

He frowned. "That bothers you?"

"No. I just want you to believe we won't be interrupted. Mae's spending the night with Char. She often does on the week-ends."

Jacques's thoughts ran in hot, dark directions. Gaby wanted and needed them to be together, alone, as much as he did. "I'm going to have to do something. I'll make it as short as I can." His parents could be long-winded and he enjoyed them too much to put them off.

Before he'd fully stopped the engine in Gaby's driveway, she was out of the Jeep and racing for the house.

Tugging his tie undone, Jacques went after her. Anticipation made itself felt in the usual way where Gaby was concerned.

He closed the door behind him and walked forward, looking for her. "Gaby? Where are you?"

"Back here." Her voice came from a passageway to the left and he saw her head poking from a room. "Come on. You won't miss a thing, I promise you."

"I believe you." Her approach titillated him. Evidently Gaby McGregor wasn't a woman practiced in setting up seductions. He breathed deeply. That suited him fine. She was, however, the kind of woman erotic dreams were made of, and to walk toward her now, knowing her intentions, made him instantly ready for what they did so well together.

The call to his parents could wait.

She pulled him into a small, softly feminine bedroom decorated in pale yellows and lavenders and furnished with white wicker. That surprised him. He'd expected the same dramatically bold colors and lines she favored in clothing.

"Get everything off."

His head snapped toward her. He smiled, and the smile broadened. "In a masterful mood, huh? Okay. I can take orders."

The tux jacket was whipped from his shoulders the instant he undid the buttons. Before he could make another move, Gaby unbuckled his cummerbund and went to work on the shirt studs.

"You understand me, Gaby. That's a rare thing." The shirt went the way of the jacket. "You know when I can wait and when I can't."

"Don't worry about a thing." She pulled off his shoes, and then his trousers hit the floor. "I'm going to take care of you, Jacques."

Yeah. "I'm sure you will," he said and heard the thickening in his own voice.

Ms. McGregor might not have had a whole lot of recent practical experience, but she stripped a man with remarkable efficiency. Seconds more and Jacques stood, stark naked except for his watch.

Gaby gathered his clothes into a pile, plunked them on the puffy bed comforter and faced him. "Into the shower with you."

"The shower?" he asked carefully. He locked his knees against the pulsing in his groin.

"Yes." Apparently oblivious to his physical reactions, she darted away into a bathroom off the bedroom, and he heard the shower come on.

Marvelously fascinated, Jacques followed and was confronted with a wholly pleasing view of Gaby's perfect derriere in the short skirt of her cotton dress. She leaned through the glass doors of the shower.

The temptation to grab and leap with her into the water wasn't easy to quell. But this was her show, and he had no doubt he'd enjoy every moment of what she had planned.

Gaby straightened and called, "Jacques!"

"Right here, honey."

She jumped and spun around. "Yes." Her eyes were wide. "Get in." The steam had turned her cheeks dewy pink. Tendrils of black hair curled about her face.

"Anything you say." He remembered his

watch and fiddled with the band. "How long will you be?"

"Not long. Not long at all. You go ahead while I see to things. I'll be quick, I promise. I know you're in a hurry."

Before he could say another word, Gaby left the bathroom. Thoughtfully Jacques puffed up his cheeks and got into the shower. She knew he was in a hurry. That didn't exactly sound romantic.

He let the water beat on his face. This whole episode was bizarre — not that he was complaining.

Seconds passed.

Jacques soaped his body. He thought back over the events since he'd left Goldstrike earlier in the evening.

He was definitely being set up.

Gaby had rushed away from the meeting in time to position herself on the road to La Place. And he'd lay odds she deliberately removed the wheel from her bike.

He rinsed off and located a bottle of shampoo.

To knock him over, she'd had to walk around the bike and into him. That had been no accident, either.

Cautiously he slid the shower door open a few inches and peered out. There was a clear view into the bedroom. Gaby wasn't there.

So, she'd waylaid him, knocked him in the dirt and wiped her muddy hands all over him, then insisted on bringing him back here and forcing him into the shower. Not that she could have forced him if he hadn't wanted to go. And, so far, she hadn't appeared — pink and creamy all over and ready to join him for the grande finale.

He lathered his hair and sloshed the soap out.

I know you're in a hurry to get somewhere important, Gaby had said.

Jacques screwed up his eyes, considering. *What time is it . . . that late? You must be beside yourself.*

Yet he'd said nothing about being on his way anywhere, or about any deadlines.

With you being in such a hurry and needing to arrive where you're going in a tux I'm sure I can fix you up quickly at my house . . . then you can be on your way and not make anyone upset or miss anything you've got to do.

Almost as if she'd known about the meeting with Napoleon and the order to wear a tux. . . .

But how —

"Hell!" The scene in his bedroom the previous Sunday played in his mind like a full-color movie. "She read the fax!"

Very deliberately Jacques finished rinsing and slicking back his hair, then he rested a shoulder against the wall and waited.

Finally a small shadow moved toward the

shower. The moment Gaby began to slide open the door, he bent his head under the water once more. "This is awful," he said. "Awful."

"Jacques?"

"That's my name. Where have you been?"

"Um, seeing to things."

He could imagine. "What time is it? I can't be late."

She cleared her throat. "It's not late."

"Not late? What does that mean? I asked you for the time."

"I'll go look."

"Don't bother." He shot out a hand and grabbed her wrist. "I've got soap in my eyes, damn it. I hate that. Ouch! It stings."

"I'll get you a wash cloth."

"It hurts! Get it out now."

Through slitted lids he saw her reach toward his face. Bracing himself, timing his move, he waited until her balance was the most precarious. "Ouch!" Feeling around, he settled his hands on her upper arms and yanked.

Her shriek brought him deep satisfaction. Two could play this kind of game, and he wouldn't botch it like some.

Gaby landed against him and held on to stop herself from sliding to the shower floor. Shock registered on her face. While her hair became plastered to her head and shoulders, her mouth opened and closed like a beached fish.

"Wow, I'm sorry," Jacques said, steadying her directly under the full force of water. "You're getting wet."

Gaby blinked and swiped at her face.

"If you don't take that dress off it's going to get ruined." The white cotton clung to every curve. He could make out the patterned lace of her bra — and peachy-colored skin beneath — and nipples puckered like irresistible little pebbles.

She made a move to get out, but he slid the door shut firmly instead. "You don't want to drip all over the floor, honey. Here, let me help you out of that thing." At least she'd taken off her shoes.

When he started unbuttoning her bodice, Gaby made an ineffectual attempt to stop him.

"Don't worry about me," he told her. "If I'm late, I'm late. I learned the importance of prioritizing a long time ago."

The bewildered expression on her face almost undid him. The sight of her breasts beneath transparent cotton and lace fried his concentration completely.

Gaby's hands slid from his chest to his hips. "Look at me. What a mess."

"I am looking," he murmured. "And what I see is anything but a mess."

"Jacques, I . . ." She looked at his mouth and her lips parted.

231

"Jacques, I what?" he asked, bending closer. "What, Gaby?"

"I . . . Kiss me, please."

With water cascading over them, he did as she asked, and did it again and again, until she clung to him and he crossed his arms around her, slid up her dress to cup her bottom through flimsy silk panties and press her hips into his.

Gaby stood on tiptoe and Jacques gasped as her ruckled dress passed over him. She used the tip of her pointed tongue to play with the corners of his mouth, reached higher and turned his head to nip at his ear. And with each move, wet fabric stimulated his already pulsing flesh.

"You are driving me insane," he told her through gritted teeth. Panting, he planted her hands firmly at her sides and held them there while he caught his breath. "Okay, okay. Don't touch me. Don't move a muscle or I'm not going to make it."

She licked at wet lips and he groaned.

"I didn't mean for this to happen." Her voice was very small. "Honestly, I didn't plan to —"

"Please — don't talk for a minute, my love. There'll be lots of time for talking . . . later."

He hadn't gotten far with his first attempt at the bodice buttons. This time he concentrated. The buttonholes seemed to have shrunk, making the operation even more tedious, but perseverance prevailed. With the last one, he parted the dress, laying open to his view a white lace bra that didn't cover the tops of her nipples and served only to turn him on even more-if that were possible.

Jacques worked the dress from her shoulders and pulled her arms from the sleeves before returning to her breasts. He slipped a finger beneath each bra cup and rubbed back and forth over her nipples.

"Jacques!" Gaby's voice rose to a squeak.

He kissed her again, still playing with the stiff nubs, still sending her writhing against him. Their mouths ground together, not quite silencing Gaby's moans.

Jacques felt her hands between them, then the bra disappeared and she guided him to cover her breasts. When she took him into her firm fingers, a jolt shot to his knees and he almost buckled.

"Lean on the wall," she ordered, pushing him back while she bent to wriggle out of the dress and panties. These she tossed behind her while taking him, for an instant, into her mouth.

Jacques heard his own yell and arched his neck.

The sensation of a small but voluptuous and totally naked body layered on his, captured his immediate, complete attention.

Gaby pulled on his shoulders. "Look at me."

"Gladly." He could look at her forever.

Slowly, sensuously, she raised a knee, drew her leg up his thigh. "Come on, Jacques. Come *on*."

Smiling, he lifted her and she wrapped her legs around his waist. "You may be the death of me yet, lady." He changed their places to rest her against the tile.

"If I don't go first," she said.

"How about both going together?"

The rest was accomplished in silence but for the sound of pelting water and labored breath. And in the end it took everything Jacques had not to fall to his knees.

Finally Gaby said, "Who needs horseback? We do just fine all on our own."

"Fine," Jacques murmured against her cheek. "But if I don't get out of this shower and lie down, I'm going to keel over." He turned off the water.

"Me, too."

They stumbled through the bathroom to the bedroom. Jacques stripped back comforter and sheet and fell onto the bed with Gaby in his arms. "We're getting this wet."

"Who cares?"

"Are you sure Mae's not likely to show up?"

"Absolutely sure."

"Gaby, you are really something. I'm never

going to get enough of you."

She had grown still.

Jacques shook her gently and tipped her face up to his. "You okay?"

She kept her eyelids lowered. "Yes. But I'm ashamed."

"Of what?"

"I played a trick on you."

He'd almost forgotten! "Why don't you tell me about it? Then I'll decide how angry to be with you."

"I put your tux in the dryer. It'll be all wrinkled. And it probably shrank, too."

"Why would you do a thing like that?" He wanted to grin so badly his face hurt.

"Your shirt's in the washer. It's wet now."

"You said you could clean me up in no time."

"I lied."

She was wonderful. And she was useless as a schemer. Jacques managed to appear disturbed.

"Do you know what time it is?" Gaby asked. "Look at the clock behind me."

"Nine-forty. That late? Boy, doesn't time fly when you're having fun."

"Jacques, I can't pretend and lie anymore. I'm no good at it. I knew you had to race back to La Place to meet with Napoleon Paradise at nine this evening. I set out to make you miss your appointment and I've done it."

Her fingers dug into his chest. He eased

them away and held her hands.

A defiant light entered her wonderful eyes. "I'm not sorry you didn't make the meeting. But the way I did it was wrong."

"Yes it was," he told her solemnly.

"I didn't mean to — What just happened wasn't part of the plan."

"It should have been."

"All I intended to do was get you dirty and make you too late."

"Gaby, Gaby, that wasn't nice." Scooting them upward onto the pillows, he pulled the sheet up as they went.

"I was desperate. And you've been manipulating me. I know about the leprechaun auditions on the weekend you told me you wanted us to go to LA."

"Is that a fact?" He was getting aroused again. With exaggerated care he pushed Gaby onto her back and, very deliberately, stroked her breasts.

"Jacques! Aren't you hearing a word I'm saying?"

"Every one." The tip of his tongue, applied to a nipple, brought a very satisfactory response. Gaby's knees jackknifed and she filled her fingers with his hair. "I do believe you like this," he said, opening his mouth to suckle.

"You can't be ready again. Not this soon."

"Want to bet?"

"No."

He smiled and ran a hand down her

stomach. "Why, I do believe I'm not the only one who's ready."

"Jacques, aren't you mad at me? That crazy Paradise man will be furious. He'll probably refuse to reschedule the appointment."

"You, my love, shouldn't read other people's fax messages. When I was driving into Goldstrike this evening I got a call on the car phone."

"You did?"

"Yep. Napoleon canceled until further notice."

15

A week hadn't done a thing to lessen her embarrassment. No, Gaby told herself, she would never, *never*, recover from the awful discovery that not only had Napoleon Paradise put off his visit before she knocked Jacques to the ground and crawled all over him, but that Jacques had *guessed* exactly what she'd been doing . . . *before* he'd yanked her into the shower.

She left the sidewalk in front of her showroom and crossed the street on her way to buy coffee.

Char couldn't understand why Gaby had told Jacques she never wanted to see him again!

The grayness of the day matched her mood. November had never been a favorite month and this one was worse than any she remembered.

Why had he given up *trying* to get her to talk to him? She might have changed her mind the next time he called or stopped by.

"Gaby! Wait!"

If there'd been any alternative, she'd have

slipped away. Unfortunately there was no question of pretending not to see Sophie rushing into her path.

"I was hoping to find you," Sophie said, catching up. "I'd have been along earlier only there was a meeting about the new library."

Gaby halted. "I haven't heard anything about a new library."

"No. Well . . . You have been a bit distant for the past few days, dear." The wind carried wisps of Sophie's white hair forward. "Anyone would think you were avoiding all of us."

"Tell me about the library," Gaby said, feeling belligerent.

Sophie waved a hand. "It's to be part of the senior center that's being built."

Another Ledan sop to the populace reared its head. "And where will that be? What will we lose to get it?"

"I'm sure I don't know. And I don't know what you're suggesting, either. You're upset, Gaby. Come along. We'll take a walk and talk about what it is that's making you so nasty."

"I am *not* nasty!"

"No, dear." Sophie threaded her arm through Gaby's and began to walk determinedly down the street. "You are too hard on yourself, dear. Really you are."

Gaby wrinkled her nose. *Dear* had never

been in Sophie's vocabulary. "I don't have time for this. I was on my way to buy some coffee. We're almost out."

"The coffee can wait."

"We're in full production for a show, Sophie."

"And you can't produce without coffee?"

"In my business people have to be happy to work well."

Sophie continued on without missing a step. "In that case you must be working very poorly indeed."

"All right." Gaby planted her feet. "What exactly is this all about? Who's been talking to you and what have they said? Did Mae tell you I've been short-tempered? Is that it?"

"No." Sophie's cheeks turned pink. "Sit with me." She indicated a bench in front of the defunct Goldstrike Exotic Pet Emporium.

Graceful surrender could sometimes be the best course. Gaby sat down and Sophie joined her.

"Do you call that thing you're wearing a boater?" Sophie asked.

"Yes." She tilted the straight brim of her shiny straw hat lower over her eyes.

"Sort of a W. C. Fields effort. Interesting, I suppose. I'm not sure about the yellow-green color on you, though. And I do think dried prunes are a bit much."

"They're big blackberries."

"Are they? Well that's the problem, then.

You should have made them the right size so they wouldn't look like prunes."

Gaby had to smile. She shook her head and slid to slouch into the back of the bench. "You aren't interested in hats or blackberries or prunes, Sophie. You're hedging. Get to the point."

"Oh, dear. Was I being rude?"

"Sophie?"

"Yes, well . . . Well, I don't know why I'm prattling like this. I expect old age is finally settling in."

Commenting that old age had usually set in by one's late seventies didn't seem kind.

"Anyway, I just wanted to tell you that I don't agree with Char. Not one bit. There. Now I've said it."

Gaby crossed her arms. "Char said something about me? Something you don't agree with?"

A fit of genteel coughing delayed Sophie's response. Then she said, "I'm sure Char's only worried in case Mr. Ledan takes advantage of you — again, that is."

If a caterpillar had climbed a nearby leaf, Gaby would have heard it. She felt aware of every tiny sound and movement in the world. Her mouth had dropped open but she didn't care. Even Char, who said almost anything to almost anyone, wouldn't share Gaby's personal humiliation — and most private encounters — with *Sophie.* Straight-laced

241

Sophie who'd lived a spinster's life in an age when that meant *virginity!*

"You can rely on me for discretion, Gaby. You're a nice girl. Whatever you've done, I'm certain it's been with the good of the cause in mind. You decided to sacrifice yourself for the sake of others." Sophie raised her chin and drew her shoulders back. "I, for one, applaud your unselfishness."

Listening to a caterpillar climbing was fodder for novices. Now Gaby could have heard flowers growing at the seed stage — if it weren't for the blood roaring in her ears. Her cheeks throbbed.

"Look at you, you poor little thing." Sophie pried one of Gaby's hands free and clasped it between both of her own. "Beaten down by the weight of all the responsibility that's been thrust upon you. Is it your fault you were the one Mr. Ledan singled out as a friend? Is it?"

Gaby shook her head.

"Of course it isn't. And I think that to have the courage to go out there on that road and as good as *throw* yourself in front of that unpleasant vehicle he drives was nothing short of *heroic.*"

Char *had* told Sophie. Gaby covered her face.

"Oh, my, you *are* upset. I'm not doing this very well, I'm afraid. What I should be saying is that I don't think things are going to work out at all badly . . . in general, that is."

"Things couldn't be worse."

"That's not true. Look, I want you to consider something. Promise me you will."

Gaby couldn't bring herself to look at Sophie. "I can't promise to do something when I don't know what it is." As soon as she could get away she'd hide and never come out. She was *mortified.*

"You made wonderful progress with Mr. Ledan."

"Can't we let this — wonderful progress?"

"Absolutely." A delighted smile made Sophie look younger. "I know all about that horrid Napoleon Paradise person. I looked him up and he's a disaster. He'd *be* a disaster in Goldstrike. That's what we've got to stop at all costs — the theme park."

"And the gambling excursions to Tahoe, the high-rise luxury hotel and the health spa," Gaby muttered.

"Yes, of course. But first things first. And you've made a start, you clever thing. You got Mr. Ledan to put off Mr. Paradise's visit indefinitely!"

"I didn't —"

"Stop belittling your efforts, Gaby. You didn't get Mr. Ledan to abandon the park entirely — yet. But before you made your superb effort, the whole thing was in motion."

Effort? Gaby hadn't had a migraine in years. Today might be the day to break that happy record. "Char told you about my . . . effort with Jacques."

"She certainly did. And she said she'd warned you it wouldn't do any good. Men, she informed me in that terribly flip way of hers, will always be flattered by that sort of thing — enjoy it, I think she said, but not be swayed from a decision already made. But she's being foolish because — obviously — your effort did sway Mr. Ledan. Somewhat."

"I see." Why burst Sophie's bubble?

"Yes. And the reason I wanted to talk to you this morning — in addition to congratulating you on what you've already accomplished — was to ask you to do something else for us."

"Something else?" Gaby said weakly.

Sophie swiveled and regarded her seriously. "I'll understand if you think this is too much."

"What is it?"

"Try again, Gaby. Maybe this time you'll be completely successful and Mr. Ledan will decide to give up on the theme park. For the good of the cause, I'm asking you to repeat your effort."

There was nothing to be said. No answer could convey Gaby's amazement. She stared into Sophie's sincere blue eyes and felt her own muscles turn to water. Sophie Byler, spinster and ex-schoolteacher, upholder of upstanding morals and president of the Women's Auxiliary had exhorted Gaby to venture once more to seduce Jacques Ledan!

"It was a risk," Sophie said. "I knew it, but I took it, anyway. I hope you won't think less of me."

Feeling shell-shocked, Gaby pushed her hat to the back of her head. "I don't think less of you. How could I?"

"Because I was selfish enough to push you too far."

"Nothing could push me farther than I've already been pushed this week."

"Nevertheless . . ." Sophie became silent and her grasp on Gaby's hand tightened. "Oh, my. Some things simply are not fair."

Gaby looked at Sophie, then slowly turned to see what had drawn the old lady's lips into a disapproving line.

Striding down the center of the street, his denim duster flying in dashing Western fashion, came a tall, huskily-built man.

A weak sun chose that moment to spear through the clouds, and Gaby shaded her eyes. The man's face was in shadow, but his thick blond hair, worn rakishly long, shone — especially where hours on some California beach had turned it almost white.

His shoulders swung and the heels of his silver-toed, gray snakeskin slouch boots rang on the pavement.

A way behind him, parked a distance from the curb, stood a white Mercedes convertible with the top down.

He arrived in front of them.

Gaby started at the custom boots, worked her way up gray leather jeans that fitted athlete-perfect legs like a second skin, skimmed past a low-slung belt of solid silver links, a gray silk shirt of flamboyantly Western cut and arrived at the newcomer's square jaw.

The sun made another run for it.

"Hi, Gab," the man said. "Gorgeous as ever, babe. You never change."

"Neither does he," Sophie murmured.

Of course the chin had a cleft just deep enough to be irresistible. The lips that parted in a smile showed white teeth that had never needed bonding.

Warm, boyishly honest eyes were pure, cerulean blue and fringed with thick, black lashes.

Standing in the middle of Goldstrike on a November afternoon was a man no woman could fail to run her car into a pole for.

Gaby plucked at a hole in one leg of her jeans and spread an arm along the back of the bench. "And I said nothing could push me farther than I'd already been pushed this week. Hello, Michael."

He'd made up his mind to stay away from her.

"You do know who Michael Copeland is, don't you?"

Jacques paced another circuit around a storeroom behind the building that housed his suite and Gaby's business premises. Char Brown had called with an urgent request for him to meet her there. Now she was telling him things he didn't want to hear.

"I said —"

"*Yes,* of course I know who he is. He's some costume designer from Hollywood."

"Oh, boy."

"Do you want to enlarge on that?"

Char shrugged, drawing her thin shoulders up into wild, graying black curls. "My father never taught me much, but he was pretty insistent that it's more important to know your adversaries well than your friends moderately well."

"I think I can decode that. You're telling me I don't have Michael Copeland's number. And you're also telling me he's my adversary."

"Something like that."

"Well you're wrong on at least one count. The man means nothing to me."

"Good. Every time he comes to Goldstrike he upsets Gaby."

Jacques swung around. "How?"

"I thought you didn't care about him."

"I don't. I asked how he upset Gaby."

She smiled, and wrinkles fanned into the brown skin of her face. "And you do care about her, don't you?" She motioned him to remain silent. "Michael's a big, talented kid. That's why he didn't want children. He couldn't cope with the idea of not holding center stage at all times — with Gaby as well as with everyone else."

"He loved her?" Jacques disliked the way his stomach squeezed.

"As much as he could love anyone but himself. He did come to love Mae, too, but by then it was too late for him and Gaby. Oh, he tried to get her back. She was too smart. If she wasn't such a mush heart, she wouldn't let him see Mae at all, but she thinks it's important for the child to know her father. And, if the truth were known, she thinks it's good for him to spend time with Mae."

"Children should know both their parents," Jacques said distractedly. "Do you know why he's here now?"

"Ostensibly to check progress on the hats for *Going to the Dogs.*"

He looked at her sharply. "You think there's another reason?"

"Yes. I think he's gotten wind of you through the grapevine — namely Mae. He's probably come to check you out. If Gaby doesn't want him anymore, he doesn't want her to want anyone else."

"The man's sick."

"Not really," Char said. "Just the product of his environment. He's been adored for so long, he can't adjust to losing any part of his entourage. I doubt if he's even conscious of what he's doing."

"But he makes Gaby unhappy?"

"He unsettles her by trying to send her on a guilt trip for not letting him back into her life."

Jacques lifted his face to the sky. So, the creep who'd left Gaby when she was pregnant had showed up because he was afraid she might finally be taking someone else into the place he'd once occupied.

"What do you think I ought to do?" Not that he intended to do anything.

"It doesn't really matter what I think." Char smoothed her loose, orange cotton skirts. "I'd better get back. But I did think you'd like to know she's with him over at Sis's and, unless I don't know her as well as I think I do, she's feeling pretty miserable."

16

Laughter — and a rush of hot air — met Jacques as he walked into Sis's.

He slid quietly onto the nearest counter chair. Not that he need worry about intruding on the raucous company. The motley band crowded into the center of the diner hadn't noticed Jacques's arrival.

"It was a blast!" A man's strong voice rose above the others as he stood talking to the group. *Hollywood* might as well have been written on his broad, gray silk-clad chest. His fascinated audience listened intently.

"Hoffman walked out, of course," the man said, pushing a hand into tousled blond hair. "But what else is new? What a hell of a party, though. Hey —" he pointed to Barney from the Hacienda "— have you seen Julia's new do?"

Barney shook his head.

"Be grateful," the orator announced. "She should have stuck with her old look, and I'm not the only one who's told her so." The man's other hand rested on the back of Gaby's neck. She sat, the only unsmiling member of the group, with her gaze firmly trained on her lap.

A light touch on Jacques's back made him look over his shoulder — and into Char Brown's sharp eyes. "Do I need to introduce anyone to you?"

Muscles in Jacques's jaw twitched. "I didn't hear you come in."

"I wonder why. What do you think of Michael?"

"Think?" He drummed the counter. "Nothing. I guess, except that I hate the SOB." The vehemence in his words didn't put a crack in the black tension that mounted in his gut.

"Gaby was very young when they met. So was he. The difference is, she grew up." Char spoke through barely parted lips. "Oh-oh. You're on. She's seen you."

The instant Jacques looked into Gaby's eyes, his view was cut off by Sis who proceeded to pour coffee all around. But the instant had been long enough for him to see, first unhappiness, then embarrassment. He understood both and hated that he was responsible for the latter. If he'd used his damned head he would never have told her he knew what she'd set out to do on Saturday. Gaby accused him of using her, of making love to seal her humiliation.

You've enjoyed making a fool of me, haven't you? she'd told him. And those had been her

251

parting words when she'd insisted he leave her house.

"Mr. Ledan!"

Jacques's name, yelled in her ear by Caleb, jolted Gaby all the way to her toes. She felt the entire company's attention shift in the direction of the tall, darkly silent man at the counter.

"Mike," Caleb continued in a bellow. "You gotta meet Mr. Jacques Ledan. He's the one who's putting little old Goldstrike on the map. Gonna see to it that our kids get to go to school here in town again and that there's enough work to keep 'em here when they're through. The two of you are bound to have a heap in common — both of you bein' movers, like they say."

Gaby felt Michael's fingers tighten on her neck. As if she watched a scene without sound acted out on the other side of a glass wall, she saw him lean forward across heads, his right hand extended, and saw Jacques rise smoothly from his chair and approach.

Nothing in common, she wanted to shout. But they wouldn't have heard on their side of the glass. *These two men are different from the bone out.*

Jacques wore all black as he had that first day in her showroom. And today, as then, flecks of black showed in his searingly blue eyes, eyes that looked not at Michael, whose hand he shook, but at Gaby.

"The candy man himself," she heard Michael say in his best, deliberately hearty voice. "Great to meet you, Jacques. Heard a whole lot about you. And I'm excited about what you represent to these folks. Hell, I'm amazed someone hasn't come along and seen what there was to be made here long before this. Trust a man who turns sugar into you-know-what to see gold in dirt."

Only Michael's grip on her neck stopped Gaby from jumping up.

Jacques's flat gaze would have closed most men's mouths permanently.

"Hey," Michael said, slapping his thigh. "Gold from dirt in Goldstrike. They sure as hell never found much of the real stuff when they were looking for it. Took a French taffy puller to do the job. Pretty good, huh, Jacques?"

The slow movement that caught Gaby's eye was Jacques's hand, curling into a fist at his side. "We're third-generation Californians," he said quietly.

"Hello, Michael," Char popped from behind Jacques. "Why didn't you call and say you were coming, you reprobate?"

"I knew I'd be welcome." Michael laughed. He swept up an arm. "And I was right, wasn't I, folks?"

A chorus of assent followed.

"And you know you keep a bed made up

for me, Char, love." He blew her a kiss. "I'll be over later."

"Come and join us, Jacques. Pull up a chair. Sis! Bring Jacques here a cup of coffee."

Jacques didn't move.

"It's nice to see you, Mr. Ledan," Sophie said politely from her seat, which was slightly removed from the rest. "I've already explained about the library and the senior center. Everyone is most appreciative, I assure you."

Gaby closed her eyes tightly and opened them again. Sophie was deferring to Jacques, just as Caleb already had.

"Mighty nice," Sis said, in a remarkably clear voice. She smiled at Jacques with frank friendliness. "And my brothers say the teen center is goin' to mean nothin' but good to me — with me supplyin' the refreshments at the concession stand, that is."

Jacques appeared vaguely uncomfortable, but he nodded at Sis and the others. "We'll make a great team."

"I really am flattered that you want me to help draft a proposal to the state about the school," Sophie put in.

They were defecting. Gaby managed to shrug away from Michael's hand. One by one, everyone in the town was going over to Jacques's side because all they could see was what they, personally, had to gain. Even

Sophie, who had been so adamantly opposed to the whole project, had drawn back and dumped the problem of the theme park in Gaby's lap as the apparent sole remaining adversary.

The door flew open to reveal Camilla Roberts. "Hello, everybody," she said loudly, but managing to retain the huskily sexy quality in her voice. "I'm *so* excited! Is it true?"

It was happening. Everything she'd feared. This town was turning into a glitzy zoo. Gaby tried to gauge an inconspicuous escape.

"Hi, Jacques," Camilla said. "Why didn't you tell me *the* Michael Copeland was in town?"

"When would I have done that?"

"Oh, *you*. Such a tease. I swear, if Rita hadn't taken me in, I'd be having no fun at all on my vacation."

"I thought you were just passing through town," Jacques commented without looking at Camilla. "This is Michael Copeland. He's passing through, too."

Gaby eyed him sharply, but saw no sign of anger — or of any emotion at all.

"Michael Copeland," Camilla said breathily and with great reverence. "If you knew how I've dreamed of this moment. I'm Camilla Roberts."

"It's great to meet you, Camilla," Michael said. He drew up another chair — on the other side of him from Gaby — and motioned

Camilla into it. "Sit right here and tell me about yourself."

Gaby's head jerked up so sharply, her neck cracked. After all these years nothing about Michael had changed. A beautiful, fawning woman still made him react like a grateful dog in the mating season.

"I can't believe it." Camilla slid to sit beside Michael who promptly found a new neck upon which to lavish attention. "I can't. I've wanted to meet you for just ages. For *ever*. I'm a makeup artist, you know. Ask Jacques."

Michael wasn't asking anyone anything. "I'd have known that without being told. You look wonderful, baby. Who're you working for these days?"

"Well." Camilla, in a thigh-high, gold satin shirt-dress with buttonholes that were evidently too small to use, crossed one long, bare, tanned leg over the other and fixed her big, brown eyes on Michael. "Actually I'm between engagements. I was considering an offer from Jacques to oversee things at his little spa, but my real love is — *naturellement* — the movies!" She squealed.

"God, this is something," Michael said, dropping into a crouch beside Camilla. "I knew I'd heard your name. Camilla Robertson, *the* makeup artist."

"Roberts. You've *heard* of me?"

"You bet I have, baby." Michael's eyes were in great position to figure out how much bigger Camilla's buttonholes needed to be. "And I'm into a big deal right now. A *big* deal. *Going to the Dogs.* You've heard of it?"

Another squeal rent the air.

"Right. Well, of course, I get mucho input in your chosen area, sweetie. Leave it to me. I'll work something out — if you'd like that."

"Oh, I like. I like very much."

Michael draped an arm around Camilla's shoulders. "Consider it done." He tore his gaze from the region of Camilla's buttonholes and inclined his head to Gaby. "Gaby's doing the hats — to my specs, of course. Isn't that right, love?"

Gaby seethed. "The movie's going to be wonderful. An extravaganza." True, Michael was a genius at what he did, but where hats were concerned he'd always deferred to her.

"Did you know Gaby's my wife?" Michael continued. "Ex-wife, that is. We're one of those lucky couples who came through a divorce as the best of friends. Isn't that right, love?"

She'd dearly love to slap him. "We manage."

"Which brings me to another point," Michael said, bouncing to his feet and jabbing a finger in Jacques's direction. "I understand my ex has a new man-of-the-moment. I'd have thought she'd make sure I was the first to know about a thing like that, wouldn't you, Camilla?"

Camilla, wisely, said nothing.

"Is it true that you've got the hots for my little Gaby, Jacques?"

Gaby looked at the floor and felt her face turn dull, throbbing red. "Michael," she whispered. "Please don't."

He wrapped his arms around her. "You know I'm a joker, love. I don't want anything but the best for you. That's why it's my duty to make sure what's what where you're concerned."

"And where Mae's concerned, too?"

A second passed before he laughed. "Of course. That doesn't have to be said."

"None of this has to be said."

"Jacques," Michael boomed. "Isn't this *some* woman I used to be married to!"

"She certainly is," Jacques agreed.

"God!" Michael slapped a hand to his brow. "I just had a fantastic idea . . . one of many I have every day. Didn't I hear you were planning a movie theater here?"

"Eventually."

"Well, hell. Why not *use* everything that comes easily to hand? Why not a live theater, too?"

Jacques raised one brow. "I suppose —"

"Of course! Production would be no sweat. I could send appropriate material your way — and even let you use part of my team for costumes and sets from time to time. But, best of all, we could put our heads together and find ways to showcase Gaby's stuff." He grinned at her. "Don't thank me, love. What are old friends for? Right, Jacques?"

"I always try to separate business and pleasure myself."

She heard Jacques's voice through the pulse thundering in her ears.

"By the way," Michael said. "It's time I asked the big question."

Jacques hooked his thumbs into his pockets. "Which is?"

"Why, what exactly are your intentions toward my ex-wife, of course? After all, I do have an interest in these matters."

"Intentions?" Jacques laughed, and Gaby felt her blood pressure rise. "Who said I had any?"

The distance to the door was too long. Gaby's legs moved as if through deep water until her hand closed on the handle.

"Wait for me." Jacques held her elbow. "We've got things to talk about."

Gaby looked at his fingers on her arm, then at his face. "Tell me, Jacques Ledan, do you know what they call men like you?"

She saw his pupils dilate, his mouth open slightly.

"I see you do. Unfortunately, you give all the other spineless bastards a bad name."

17

"This is crazy, Gaby," Rita said. "How do you stand it?"

"I thrive on chaos. Most people in my business do — those who get into the theatrical stuff."

All work stations in the room were occupied. Brilliantly colored materials littered every surface, echoing the shades used in sketches pinned to boards around the walls.

"Gaby," Char called. The day's mail littered the desk in front of her. "This is the rent check. It's been returned."

Gaby massaged her aching neck. "Is the address right on the envelope?"

"It's preprinted."

"Then it makes no sense. Call and say we'll get it to them."

"Tell me how you got into millinery," Rita said, following Gaby from chair to chair as she resumed overlooking work in progress and made comments. "Did you get up one day when you were seven and say, 'Gee, I want to make hats' or something like that?"

Gaby didn't want to talk about her work. She didn't want to talk or think about anything. "It's a long story. I'll tell you sometime if you still feel like it. Why are you here, Rita?" The other woman had arrived more than an hour earlier and on no apparent mission.

Without warning, Rita fell into a chair and clamped her hands over her face.

All Gaby needed was a crying female on her hands. "What is it?" she asked, as nicely as possible. "Can I help?" Even if she was incapable of helping herself.

Rita dropped her hands, revealing dry eyes in a pale face with a bright spot of color on each cheek. "I have had it, Gaby. *Had* it. And I couldn't think of anyone but you who might be as fed up as I am."

Wonderful.

Char chose that moment to breeze up with a purple satin turban draped with ropes of pearls. "Can't get through to the landlord. Where the hell are the ears supposed to stick up in this thing?"

"They don't," Gaby said, more sharply than she'd intended. "They hang down. The character's a basset hound."

"I see. *Excuse* me." Char made owl eyes and sailed on her way before Gaby could apologize for her foul temper.

"*Men*," Rita said, pursing her lips. "Can you believe what complete duds they are?"

"Complete," Gaby agreed. "Total losses." So why did the fact that she'd probably never see Jacques again — apart from across a crowded room — threaten to rip her heart out?

"You were married."

Gaby started. "Yes. To Mae's father."

"Of course. How was it?"

She wanted, suddenly and desperately, to crawl away and cry. "At first it was the whole hearts and flowers thing. Champagne and music. We were wildly in love. Or I thought we were."

"But you weren't?"

"No . . . Yes. Whatever love is, I think it was there for Michael and me at the beginning."

"Hah!" Rita, in a pair of impossibly high-heeled shoes, stretched out her legs and crossed the ankles. "But *he* didn't have the staying power, did he? I know how this scenario goes. At first he was all attention. Couldn't do enough for you. Then, when the bloom was off, when you stopped putting mascara on before you brushed your teeth in the morning, then he started looking elsewhere."

Gaby frowned. "It wasn't exactly like that."

"You don't have to make excuses for him. I know what it's like to knock yourself out for a man only to have him behave as if you're invisible. Why is it that an otherwise wonderful, sexy man becomes a blind idiot the minute a woman falls in love with him?"

"Michael didn't want children." And now he'd managed to completely ruin any chance she'd had of grabbing something marvelous with Jacques. True, she'd already ruined it herself before Michael showed up — but there might have been a chance.

"I've done everything I can think of to show I'm crazy about him," Rita mumbled.

Gaby stared unseeingly at Rita's face, at her trembling lips. Without Michael's interference, Jacques's base sense of humor and lack of chivalry might never have surfaced and then she could have hoped to — She couldn't bear to think of never being with him again.

"I kind of thought you and Jacques might have something going," Rita said tentatively.

"Well, we *don't.*" And they never would again. Any man who didn't make the effort to come after her when he'd seen the state she'd been in at Sis's two days earlier wasn't worth bothering with.

"Speak of the devil," Rita said, nodding toward the showroom.

Gaby composed herself and looked around. Instead of Jacques, Michael came strolling in, his face turned away as he surveyed the women's work. "How's it going, love?"

"Great." No thanks to him. Since his arrival, she'd only seen him for minutes at a time when he'd come to pick Mae up and bring her home that first day. He'd visited the workrooms once — when she hadn't been there.

"Great as usual," he said, smiling. "You don't need much help from me or anyone else, Gaby. You're the best."

In his profile she saw a shadow of the boy she'd fallen in love with. "Thank you, Michael."

The shadow faded, and the public Michael Copeland resumed position. "Think nothing of it, love. Just stopping by to give you a pat on the back and a cheer. We'll talk in a few days."

"Where will you be in the meantime?"

"Back in LA. I'm needed. I've already said goodbye to Mae at the school. I drove over there with Camilla."

"That must have been nice." Poor Camilla. Another Michael conquest about to be dumped.

"It was. I'm giving her a lift back to LA."

Gaby crossed her arms. "A lift? That's a fresh way of announcing a new affair. I hope she gets along with *Toby.*"

"That's over." Michael faced her. "Forget me. It's you who need to look out for yourself."

Before Gaby could react, Rita gave a small, horrified cry.

"Nice mess, huh?" Gingerly Michael

touched a split at the corner of his mouth. The eye that had been hidden was puffy, with a pocket of blue swelling beneath. "Watch yourself with that man, Gab. He's an animal."

She felt behind her for the edge of a table and leaned heavily. "Jacques? Jacques did that?"

"Not without taking a lick or two himself."

"Oh, my God," Rita said distinctly. "When? *Why?*"

"The bastard jumped me. Early yesterday, it was."

Which explained why Gaby hadn't seen Michael in twenty-four hours. "Rita — is Jacques hurt?"

"Who knows? He hasn't been returning messages for two days. The last time he talked to me he was off to Sis's for some reason he didn't bother to mention."

"But you saw him yesterday morning?" Gaby rounded on Michael. "Where? And where is he now?"

"Not, how are you, Michael, you poor dear? Or, does it hurt? To which the answer is a great big *yes*. How the hell should I know where Ledan is? He jumped me, damn it. *Jumped* me when I was leaving Char's. Fortunately Camilla was in the trailer where she's staying and she looked after me."

"Very fortunate," Gaby said. "Are you telling me Jacques Ledan waited outside

Char's and attacked you without provocation?"

"Yes . . . Damn little, anyway. The man wanted me to apologize to you. He said I'd embarrassed you in front of your friends at Sis's. We both know that's a bunch of crap."

Gaby swallowed. "You did embarrass me." Why hadn't Jacques had the guts to plead her case on the spot? The probable answer hurt. He didn't want to be seen as caring enough to stand up for her. Hadn't Jacques made fun of Michael's suggestion that he was involved with Gaby?

"I wasn't about to agree to come crawling to you about something that doesn't matter a damn. I tried to give the guy a piece of free advice — good advice I've lived by, so I know it pays off."

"And Jacques repaid your kindness by punching your face? Must have been some advice."

"You bet it was. I told him a smart man never gets confused about who's the runner and who's the runnee in the male, female game. I told him men like us are always the runners, we just don't let the little women realize it. Then he hit me."

Char had silently joined the circle. Gaby looked from her set face to Rita's disgusted glare and back to Michael. "Don't ever show up in Goldstrike again without calling first. Don't ever expose Mae to any of your *friends* unless they're suitable company for a sweet, innocent little girl." She drew a deep breath. "And don't *ever* suggest that you and Jacques Ledan have a thing in common, including being men."

"Gaby —"

"Goodbye, Michael."

At first he didn't move. Then, without another word, he swept from the room.

Conversation hummed among the women working. The overhead fans whirred. Gaby and Char regarded each other unflinchingly.

"I told you," Rita said at last. "They're no good." *Jacques.* Gaby wanted to know where he was, how he was. She owed him that much for at least making a belated effort to stand up for her.

"On a sane note," Char said. "I got through to the landlord's office."

"Good."

"You won't like this, Gaby."

She bowed her head. "If it's more irritating news, save it."

"I can't. You've got a new landlord, and the message is that you're to contact him about the rent."

"Okay. You do it for me, Char. I've got to keep focused here." If that was possible after what she'd just been through.

"Gaby."

"*Yes,* Char."

"Your new landlord is Jacques Ledan. He

bought the whole building."

She raised her face slowly and said, "Damn
him. He wants to control everything. And
he's going to do it." But she wasn't giving
up. "Fine. Redirect the rent to him —
without a cover letter. If he tries to force me
out, I'll move. It's time I built a place to my
own requirements, anyway."

Char flapped the rent envelope and
stopped, holding it in mid-air. "And here
comes Mr. Bart Stanly. Why not? Everyone
else has trailed through this very busy workroom today."

"I won't talk to him," Rita said, shooting
to her feet and turning her back. "Pretend
I'm not here."

Gaby looked at the woman's tall, impos-
sible-to-ignore back and raised her eyes to
the ceiling. "See to that rent, please, Char."

"There you are," Bart said. Windblown and
handsome in jeans and a cream-colored
turtle-neck sweater that accentuated his tan,
he bore down upon Gaby, then passed her to
arrive behind Rita. "Where did you go this
morning? I woke up expecting . . . You were
gone."

Rita hunched her shoulders. Her visible
cheek turned red.

"I thought we understood each other," Bart
said. "Then, when I need you most — when we
need each other most — you run out on me."

A mumbled response was all he got.

"Sweetheart, Jacques has decided to play the Invisible Man. He's up there at La Place sending out orders, and we're supposed to be filling them. I need you."

Before she could stop them, tears sprang into Gaby's eyes. Tears of anger; they had to be. Jacques had used and abused and discarded her. And she'd been fool enough to dream that he might be falling in love. She rubbed her brow. Darn it, anyway. She'd dreamed he was falling in love with her because she'd already fallen in love with *him*.

"Rita," Bart said with a note of desperation. "Will you please look at me?"

"Why should I. All you want from me is job support."

He caught her arm. "Don't be an idiot. You know that's not all I want."

Rita wrenched away. "That and — Oh!" One heel caught a chair leg. Her arms flailed and she began to fall.

"Good lord," Bart muttered. With something resembling a football tackle, he managed to catch Rita the instant before she would have hit the floor and swing her up into his arms. "Will you stop fighting me, woman? Will you just give in and admit you love me?"

"Love you?" Rita squeaked.

"Love me, yes. Almost as much as I love you, you infuriating female." He kissed her then, slowly, so slowly that Gaby looked away and blinked back more stupid tears. Now she was jealous of Rita and Bart.

"Excuse us," Bart said after a long, not completely silent interval. "I'm taking Rita to Vegas for a couple of days. There's something we need to do there."

Gaby nodded and managed a watery smile. "Have fun. And be happy."

"I've always thought Vegas weddings were romantic," Rita said, her arms wrapped tightly around Bart's neck.

Juggling a little, Bart pulled a fat envelope from his hip pocket and thrust it into Gaby's hands. "The master had this delivered to me to give to you. See you later, kid."

When they'd gone, Char tapped Gaby's shoulder. "Let's go outside for a bit. This joint is driving me nutty."

In the courtyard behind the building, they sat, side by side, on an upturned crate beneath trailing purple bougainvillea. Today the weather had improved again and there was a warm freshness in the breeze.

"Peace," Char said, closing her eyes. "These past few weeks have been hell in some ways, haven't they?"

"Yes," Gaby agreed and added dreamily, "when they weren't heaven."

Char took one of Gaby's hands and squeezed. "You've never been a quitter. Don't quit now."

"What choice do I have?" She knew what Char meant.

"I can't believe you two won't work it out."

"We both have to want to. Jacques doesn't."

"You don't know that."

Gaby sighed dejectedly. "Do you see any sign of him coming to beg for my company?"

"He didn't let Michael get away with insulting you."

"He let him get away with it in front of half this town. And what makes you think it was my honor he was concerned with? I saw how mad he was when Michael made those cracks about him at Sis's."

Char tapped her sandals together and wriggled her toes. "You won't know exactly what's on his mind if you don't ask, will you?"

"I'm *not* running after him!"

"Not going to be the runnee, mmm?"

Gaby turned her head away. "You can't bait me with that. It's up to Jacques to make the next move."

"And he's somewhere telling himself it's up to you. So, between the two of you, you may manage to ruin a chance at something wonderful. How stupid."

"Char —"

"What did Bart give you?"

Gaby glared at Char and ran her finger beneath the flap of the brown envelope. "Probably raising my rent." She pulled out a sheaf of forms and a note.

"Well?" Char said.

"I don't understand." Gaby read and re-read the note, then looked at the papers. "A title. To this building. It's been transferred into my name."

"You're kidding." Char took the papers. "Gaby! Jacques bought it for you! He's bought the whole darn building and given it to you as a gift. I told you he was in love with you."

Gaby stared at Jacques's note until her vision blurred. "In love with me? Oh, Char, what fools women are. Jacques Ledan is just attending to business. He's cleaning up his debts." She handed over the note.

"Dear Gaby," Char read. "My turn to do something nice for you. Enjoy. Can we talk? Jacques."

"Damn him!" Gaby leapt up. "His turn to do something *nice* for me? I'm sick of his gifts to bribe me."

"I'm sure —"

"So am I sure. He's the white knight in this town now. He doesn't want me meddling with that anymore. But he also doesn't want to kiss off — Oh, Char. Why pretend. We were good together and no man wants to pass that up. He's trying to give me a building as a sop and keep me on a string he can pull when he feels like it."

She took back the title and pushed it into its envelope with the note. "Well, there's one thing Jacques Ledan can't buy — or buy off. *Me!*"

18

"You are the only female who ever understood me," Jacques told Spike. He poured food into her bowl. "Eat. One of us has to keep some strength up."

The dog sighed hugely and remained in a heap near the kitchen door.

"I know how you feel. Okay, don't eat. We'll fade away together."

He leaned on the counter and flipped through the cook's calendar. Four days. Four lousy days he'd been up here waiting for Gaby to grasp the olive branches he'd held in her direction . . . so he could reel her in.

So far, nothing.

"She'll crack," he said aloud. "She cares, I know she does. All I've got to do is wait it out. Never met a woman who could ignore her own curiosity, and she's got to be bursting with it about now."

He opened the refrigerator, stared disinterestedly at its contents and dragged out a six-pack. "Hate the stuff," he muttered. Beer was something kept for guests, but he'd given the staff paid leave until further notice, which meant no one was buying groceries and beer was the only cold drink left.

"Stay," he ordered Spike and scuffed, bare-footed, on the trek to the study.

Standing in his window aerie overlooking the road leading down through the hills, Jacques took up vigil once more. A welcome spark of glee made him grin. She *would* come. His last little gift would make quite sure of that. Either Gaby would roar up the mountain and throw the present back at him . . . or she'd roar up the mountain and throw *herself* at him.

The latter was the most likely.

Either way, the lady would become persuaded that there was nowhere else on earth she wanted to be . . . other than with Jacques.

He looked around the room. Michael Copeland might be the artist with credentials, but he couldn't have done better than Jacques Ledan in setting a scene guaranteed to win the desired responses from the desired lady.

Sympathy.

Guilt . . . guilt was great.

An irritating twinge reminded him of the cut over his right brow. He touched it lightly and grinned again. A small price to pay for knocking Copeland on his selfish ass.

White veins of light blossomed briefly in the early evening sky.

Jacques glanced upward and scowled. He'd convinced himself the only reason Gaby hadn't come earlier today was because — according to his ally, Char Brown — the work for the movie was in its final phase. But, with Char's encouragement, he'd convinced himself Gaby *would* arrive before the day was out.

A far distant rumble of thunder sounded.

If all hell broke loose with the weather she was unlikely to venture up here — particularly since it was already getting dark.

He wouldn't want her to.

Absentmindedly, he cranked a can from the six-pack and popped the top. A fire would be nice, only that would ruin the pining-away effect he'd accomplished . . . if she should just happen to make it here after all.

The next streak of lightning raced across the sky and burst like something out of a Munster movie. Jacques dropped into his chair, pulled the beer tab all the way off and flipped it, very deliberately, onto the rug.

Thunder shook the house.

And there, on a low slope, shone the headlights of an approaching car.

"Hot damn!" He swallowed some beer, shuddered and leaned forward for a better view. "There *is* a higher being!

"Keep calm, Ledan. Don't blow it." The extra rumpling he gave his hair might not be necessary, but it made him feel good. "If that isn't you, Gaby, I'm coming after you myself."

Whoever was behind those headlights was evidently in training for the Grand Prix. The beams disappeared for brief intervals, only to zip into sight again each time.

Jacques frowned. "Damn women drivers. Menace on the roads." He felt for the buttons on his old denim shirt, only to remember they were already undone. His jeans, snug and faded from a zillion washings, rode low on his hips and showed skin at the knee.

Nature sent a blue-white roman candle through the heavens, followed it in seconds with a bass blast that rattled windows, then hurled giant raindrops on the skylight and wall of windows.

He lowered his eyelids and waited. Any display of eagerness could ruin a masterful production.

Two minutes passed before Spike barked.

Jacques took his time getting out of the chair.

The front door bell rang — and kept right on ringing. A momentary pang of misgiving lived, but promptly died. She was leaning on the bell because she wanted in out of the rain. Out of the rain and into his arms.

Keeping his pace leisurely took control. He reminded himself that in the afterglow of the reunion there would be some serious ground to be covered. But first things first.

That bell needed to be changed, or discon-
nected. It drove a man nuts.

Through the glass in the front door he
could make out Gaby's shape. He closed his
eyes for an instant and gave in to the luxury
of considering Gaby's shape in detail.

The bell ceased, to be replaced by ham-
mering.

An impatient woman could be a delight to
behold — or hold. Jacques unlocked the door
and opened it slowly, keeping one hand, the
one holding the beer can, pressed to his
naked belly. "Who the hell is it?" he said,
slurring his words. "Can't a man get any
peace in his own home?"

The door, slamming into his shoulder,
knocked him backward. His heel landed on
Spike's tail and the dog yowled before flying
away in a whirl of feet and flapping ears.

"Get out of my way," Gaby said, marching
past him.

"I'm not in your way," he pointed out, but
she showed no sign of having heard him. He
bowed as she set off into the house. "Welcome to my humble abode, Your Majesty.
Honored, I'm sure."

He closed the door and told the air, "And
that, my friends, is the way it's going to be.
The lady wants war, and she shall have it.
And then *I* shall have what I want."

Gaby awaited him in the study. When he
entered he was confronted by her back as she

bent over the desk to poke among piles of used glasses, paper plates and boxes from microwavable entrees.

"How are you, sweetheart?" he asked and sighed loudly. "How's work going for the movie?"

"What is all this?" With a finger and thumb, she held up a chicken enchilada box — with the chicken enchilada, congealed, still inside. "And this?" Sole au gratin with peapods dangled from her other hand.

"Haven't you used those? They're great. Four minutes on high, turn the tray and give them another three minutes and voilà! Delicious."

"How would you know? You haven't eaten them."

He shook his head. "I know. I just haven't been hungry lately."

Gaby dropped the boxes and surveyed the room. Then she looked at Jacques, really looked at him for the first time since she arrived. "This place is a mess. Uneaten food everywhere. Garbage on the floor. What's happened to your staff?"

"Didn't feel like seeing anyone if it wasn't you." He avoided her eyes.

"I asked you about the staff," she said, only slightly less abruptly.

"They're on leave until I call them back."

"How stupid. Sulking away up here because you aren't getting your own way in everything like you usually do."

"Gaby —"

"Are you ill?" she asked sharply.

"I guess not." He gave a gallic shrug. "Not really. Not in the conventional sense. I —"

"Either you are or you aren't. You look like hell. Have you seen a doctor?"

"No," he said. She didn't exactly sound deeply sympathetic.

"When was the last time you shaved?"

"I don't remember. Yesterday. Maybe the day before. Or the day before that."

With every second the storm gathered force. Rain burst on the windows like smashed crystals fired from a giant slingshot.

Gaby stood before the dramatic backdrop, a small defiant creature in black silk with wet droplets glittering in her unbound hair.

"Can I get you something?" he asked. "Coffee? Cognac?"

"When did you eat?"

He indicated the discarded cartons on his desk. "I have tried. Sometimes you're not in the mood."

She pulled her hair forward over one shoulder and braided it rapidly. "You and I are going to talk. First I'll shovel some of this garbage out before they send in the health department. Then you're going to eat something. Then — when I'm sure you're concentrating on every word I say — we'll get things one hundred percent straight between us, Jacques."

"What's not straight?" He knew a moment's uncertainty.

"From my point of view, nothing. From yours, just about everything, I'd say. Give me that grocery sack, the one on its side with the bottles and cans falling out."

Feeling vaguely annoyed, he did as she asked. The bag was double. She pulled one from the other and proceeded, very efficiently, to sweep away the debris he'd so artfully assembled.

Jacques watched and felt every muscle in his body grow taut — in time with his resolve. As she worked, the night grew wilder. Soon any thought she might have of delivering a verbal salvo and leaving would be out of the question.

"I've missed you, Gaby," he told her. God, was that ever true.

"Don't say that," she said, continuing to gather newspapers into a pile. "Don't say or do anything to make this harder than it already is."

"Or easier?" he suggested tentatively. "Are you afraid that if I help you calm down, you won't be able to resist me anymore?"

Her head shot up. "What do you mean by that? I hate to disappoint you, Jacques, but I *can* live without . . . without . . ."

"Can you, Gaby? Do you want to?"

She swung the strap of her purse over her

shoulder. "I'm not being drawn into this kind of conversation." With the heap of papers in one arm and a bag of garbage balanced on a hip, she headed for the corridor. "Clean yourself up. Then come to the kitchen."

Jacques followed at her heels, ignoring the furious glares she aimed at him.

"Do you have any idea what you look like?" she asked when she'd disposed of the garbage. "Unshaven, disheveled and probably unwashed."

"I always wash."

"Those jeans are falling apart."

"I know. They're comfortable." He rubbed his bare middle.

"At least you could do up your shirt."

"You do it up." He approached until he'd backed her against the sink. "I haven't been myself lately. Small tasks seem beyond me."

He saw her swallow and pass a quick glance from the center of his chest to the low waist of his jeans — and below. "Gaby, let's not waste time arguing," he said softly, bringing his mouth closer to hers. "We do other things so much better."

"No!" Pushing past him, she stood in the middle of the room. "I was going to try to do this in a civilized way, but that's impossible with you."

"Do what, Gaby?" This was definitely not going as planned.

"Tell you that although you've snowed everyone else in Goldstrike, you haven't fooled me. I may have to fight you alone, but I will fight. What you're doing to our town is *wrong*."

"And you want to talk about that? Negotiate?"

"There's nothing to negotiate about in the areas that concern me. I'm going to stop you, Jacques. That's what I came up here to tell you."

"And I thought you might have come to give us a chance to talk about our future."

She frowned. "Future?"

"Yes, future. The time you and I are going to spend together. Lots of time. We could start right now."

"By having sex?" She laughed, but her voice wobbled and her hands, before she pushed them into the pockets of her dress, trembled. "And that's what you mean by our future, isn't it? Sex together whenever you decide you need a diversion?"

Women were the most infuriating creatures.

"You know that's not all I want from you."

"Yes, I do. I know you also want me to stop opposing your plans for the area. You're afraid that I might still have enough influence around here to make things difficult for you. And you don't like it if one tiny thing doesn't go according to plan."

He stared at her. Could she really have judged him that wrongly? Could *he* have

283

failed to give her a clearer picture of his feelings?

"Look, we might as well get this over with and go our separate ways," Gaby said, a suspicion of a sheen in her eyes. "I admit I may have been wrong to be so completely unyielding about everything you've proposed."

"Thanks."

"Don't be sarcastic. I'm trying to deal with this as pleasantly as possible."

"Thanks."

"Oh, you're impossible. All men are impossible."

"If you want to make me mad, lump me together with that caricature you were dumb enough to marry."

He knew his mistake as soon as the words left his mouth.

"At least Michael has the guts to say what he thinks when he thinks it. He doesn't wait in alleys and jump people when they don't expect it, just because his pride's been a bit dented."

Jacques snorted. "I didn't jump him. I confronted him in broad daylight. *He* took the first swing. All I did was defend myself. He came off worse. Too bad from his point of view."

"If you thought he was off base in what he said about me at Sis's, why didn't you say so right then? You might have done me some good."

He planted his fists on his hips. "I'll never understand women. If it hadn't been for you, I *would* have had it out with him in the diner. I was afraid of embarrassing you."

For the first time since she'd arrived, Jacques saw her determination waver. Not for long. "I came to clear everything up between us, Jacques. When I walk back out that door, you'll know exactly what's been on my mind these past few days."

"This sounds promising." All but the walking out bit.

"Good." She began to pace about the kitchen.

"Why don't we go and get comfortable somewhere?"

"Here's fine. I don't want to take too much time over this."

"Of course not." He knew, with the strength of will for which he was famous in some circles, that he would not allow this woman to leave him tonight.

Wind moaned in the firs close to the house, and branches scraped the roof.

"I've been wrong to be so unyielding about everything."

He relaxed so abruptly he almost sighed. "I knew you'd see it my way in time."

The look she gave him was confusing: a mixture of exasperation and something he couldn't decipher — unless it was anger.

"As I was saying, I shouldn't have given the immediate thumbs-down on everything you proposed. There's a lot of good here and there in the plans. Goldstrike will be better off — as long as you're not allowed to go too far." Her eyes fixed on his. "But the trouble is that you *are* trying to go too far and that's that."

He raised his chin and looked down at her. "And only your opinion counts. Only what you think can possibly be correct, is that right?"

"I *am* right."

"Naturally." His teeth came together hard. "How could I have been so foolish as to think I didn't have to get your approval at every stage?"

She pulled her purse forward, opened it and removed an envelope. "This is yours."

When he wouldn't take it, she threw the packet on the table.

"Changing the title back into your name won't be a problem. Unfortunately the dozens of flowers you've bombarded me with in the past few days were too difficult to transport up here."

"You don't like flowers?"

"I love them." Again she didn't look away quickly enough to hide the glimmer of tears. "But not as weapons against me."

Jacques frowned. "Gaby, I don't understand you."

"You're impossible," she said.

"And you're off the wall. The most unconventional woman I've ever met."

"You're criticizing me."

"Good God." He made a grab for her and missed as she dodged out of his way. "This is pointless. Why can't —"

"You've got it! Pointless! And you can't *buy* me, Jacques." With that, she produced a set of car keys. "Having that car delivered this morning was your biggest mistake — your final mistake. If I wanted a car, I'd buy one. Maybe not a convertible Jag, but who needs one. Money isn't something I'm short of."

His temper frayed to breaking point. "But you're short of the things that really matter, Gaby."

She shook her head. "This is getting us nowhere. Keep your building. And keep your fancy car. Go back where you belong — with the rich and smooth — and leave us alone."

"Just like that? I thought you said much of what I'm doing here is worthwhile."

"I did. And it is. But you can do all of that without ever having to lay eyes on me —" breath sobbed in her throat "— and without my having to see you. But I'll fight you on the rest, Jacques. I promise you that. If it takes every penny I've got and every ounce of energy, I'm going to stop that damn theme park from being built here. And the spa. And the high-rise hotel with the shuttles to Tahoe. I'm going to stop you. Period."

He caught the keys she threw at him.

"Goodbye, Jacques. There's a lot about you I like —" her mouth worked "— a lot. Goodbye."

"No. Not goodbye," he stated flatly. "Never goodbye."

"I'm going home."

He looked at the keys in his hand. "Really. How?"

She looked momentarily nonplussed. "Um . . . you'll drive me, of course."

Jacques tossed the keys on the table. "Like hell I will."

"This is the last thing I'll ask of you."

"As far as I can remember you've never asked for anything before. But the answer's no."

"You've got to." The alarm in her eyes troubled Jacques, but what happened to-morrow and the next day — and for the rest of tonight — hinged on how he managed this little crisis.

"I don't have to do anything, Gaby. I'm going to light a fire in the study and pour us some brandy. It's wild out there. Too dan-gerous for anyone to be driving those moun-tain roads."

"I'm going home."

"No, you're not. You're going to talk things through with me. Then, when the storm passes over . . . then, we'll see."

"Jacques!"

He walked out of the kitchen and back to the study. She was headstrong, but he was about to show her he could be stronger when necessary.

The lights flickered twice while he piled wood into the fireplace. Jacques smiled. He could think of worse things than being marooned in a dark, very comfortable house with Gaby McGregor.

Flames shot up the chimney and he sat on his heels. The door slid open, but Spike rather than Gaby appeared, and came to lie close to the hearth. "Smart girl," he said, patting her. "You know when to take advantage of a good thing."

He pulled a chair close and sat down to outwait Gaby.

When the lights went out completely, he was still waiting.

More minutes passed. And more.

"Damn." Rather than come to him, she'd stand on her own in a dark kitchen. She had to be the most stubborn female he'd ever encountered . . . and the most desirable.

He negotiated his way to find her by instinct.

The wind wailed now, and rain beat each skylight as he walked beneath. At least the thunder had passed over.

As he entered the kitchen, cold air hit his face.

"What the hell . . . ?" Jacques stood still and peered around and while he did, the door to the outside batted back and forth under the onslaught of the weather.

He only hesitated a moment. "Damn fool woman." Despite the danger, she'd decided to make the return drive in the middle of the kind of storm any idiot would avoid.

Running, registering his lack of shoes but knowing every second counted, he dashed outside and around to the entrance courtyard.

The Jaguar stood where she'd left it.

Jacques, his shirt already plastered to his body, searched in all directions.

She'd set off, in driving rain and ripping wind, to *walk* home!

He couldn't go after her barefoot.

The minutes it took to return for the keys to the Jag and to pull on shoes were too long. By the time he started the powerful engine and drove from the courtyard, peering through the drenched windshield, his heart felt lodged in his throat. It would be possible to trip and fall from the edge of this road in daylight. At night, in blinding rain, it might be harder not to fall.

Crawling, ducking and straining to catch any movement, he steered around one bend after another. She couldn't have gone far.

The nose of the Jag straightened out of a curve and the headlights picked up something pale. Jacques set his teeth in a furious grimace. Then he heard a growling sound.

From the corner of his eye he saw the shape of Gaby's face whirling back in the direction from which she'd come, and the flash of her arms and legs as she started to run — toward the car.

The growling became a rumble.

Rockslide!

"Damn!" He slammed on the brakes, killed the engine and threw open his door. "Run!"

She barreled into him the instant he cleared the Jag's swinging door. "Get out of the way, Jacques! Quick! They'll hit you!"

Jacques clutched her to him and ran. The roar of falling rocks continued. A scatter of pebbles rose up the road in front of them like a gray-white rim of surf.

He stumbled. "Hold on to me!" The fine rocks worked like a runaway conveyer belt beneath his feet.

Then, as quickly as the fall had begun, it stopped. Panting, Jacques drew to a halt and, holding Gaby to him, looked back.

"Oh, my God," he murmured. "You might have been killed."

Around his body, beneath the shirt, he felt her hands creep over his skin until she could hug him with more strength than she should have had.

The Jag's headlights still shone on the pile

of rubble that covered the road. The main part of the slide had been farther on. The edge of the heap formed a wall in front of the car with scree broadcast many yards up-hill.

Jacques rested his chin on top of Gaby's head. "Now I know how a parent feels when a kid runs across the road and almost gets killed."

"You do?"

"Yeah. I'd like to shake you till your teeth raffle." Her attempt at a laugh was pathetic. She shook steadily.

"Did you honestly think you could walk all the way home?"

"No. I knew you'd come after me. Then you wouldn't have any choice but to drive me home."

"Is that a fact?" He looked down into her face. "You think you know how I'll react that well?"

"Yes," she whispered.

"Are you going to cry on me?"

"I never cry."

"Why was it so important to get home, Gaby?" He remembered Mae. "Damn, why didn't you remind me about Mae?"

"That wasn't it. She's spending the night with her new best friend, Mary-Alice Healy."

"The pain? The kid she hates?"

Gaby chuckled. "That was before Short-cake. Mary-Alice loves Shortcake and Mae's being magnanimous enough to share. You've made quite a conquest in my little girl."

"And she's made quite a conquest in me. But her mother's made more of a conquest." Carefully, reluctantly, he removed Gaby's arms, took her hand and led her back to the car.

"We'll have to wait for morning to find a way down," he told her when they were settled.

"I'm sorry, Jacques," Gaby said. "I'll try to stay out of your way till then."

The hurricane lamp Jacques had lighted for Gaby before going to the shower cast leaping light and shadow over the walls of the sitting room next to his bedroom.

She took a last look at the chart he'd left with her. "Your opinion is very important to me," he'd said. "Look this over and tell me what you think."

It was perfect. That's what she thought. The primarily final plans he'd had drawn up offered Goldstrike the best of his ideas and saved the town from the worst. He needn't think she couldn't figure out that with his outrageous gift of a Jaguar, he'd set a trap to draw her up here where he could present his plan like a boy with a perfect report card.

Gaby rolled up the chart. She'd already showered and was dressed in the top of a pair of red satin pajamas Jacques laughingly told her had been a gift from his flamboyant French mother.

Off the sitting room was a small, glassed-in porch. Gaby let herself out and crossed the wooden floor to stand staring at the sky. The rain had stopped and, behind bands of smoke-black cloud, a hint of blue moonlight shone.

"There you are." Closing the door to the sitting room behind him, Jacques came to stand beside her. With one towel he rubbed his hair. A second towel draped his hips. "What do you think? Will the plans pass, or should I find a place to hide?"

"Why didn't you just tell me what you'd done?" she asked. "I even like the idea of the rustic hotel. It'll be perfect. And the golf course. A low-key destination resort is exactly right here. People will love a chance to get an idea what life was really like in a gold rush town. I can even see the dude ranch fitting in really well. You've got such clear vision, Jacques."

He bent over and laughed.

"What's funny?"

Still laughing, he staggered to drop into a chaise. "Not so long ago you called me a man of vision and managed to make it sound like an insult. Boy, how times change."

Gaby slid open a window and shivered a little. "They sure do." She felt an air of waiting. "What will you do next, Jacques? Is it back to candy and more candy, or will you be off on another quest to improve something?"

He was quiet for a moment. "I'm not sure. . . . Ouch! Oh, ouch!"

"What is it?" Gaby hurried to his side. "What's the matter?"

"This darn cut over my eyebrow. I must have opened it up again."

"Let me see." Bending over him, she raised his face and peered to see the wound. "It's hard to see anything. But I don't think it's bleeding."

"Are you sure?" His hands rested on her hips.

"Sure."

The silence that fell seemed filled with the beating of her heart.

"Gaby, what do you want? For the future?"

I want you. She hesitated. "I'm not sure." A lie, but she didn't dare risk telling the truth.

Jacques was quiet for a long time. "You surprise me."

Gaby stepped away from Jacques and went to stand with her arms crossed on the rim of the open window. The cold breeze felt good.

She didn't hear Jacques get up. When he settled his hands on her shoulders she jumped.

"I think you do know what you want."

This time her heart turned. "What's that?"

His touch shifted, ran the length of her. He stood against her, tucked his fingers beneath the pajama top and smoothed the fronts of her thighs.

"Jacques?"

Skimming his fingertips upward, he feathered her tummy until she jerked back against him. Then he pressed down toward the center of her — until she gasped and tossed her head.

"You want what I want. We're going to have to be together, Gaby. Why fight it?" Swiftly he undid the top and tested the weight of her breasts. "I'll do the things I have to do. You'll do the things you have to do."

Gaby closed her eyes. He flipped his thumbs back and forth over her nipples, and white heat blasted all the way to her sagging knees.

"You make it sound simple." And she wanted to believe it could be. Could she be content waiting for him to come from time to time, to share the loving from time to time — until he decided not to come anymore?

He didn't speak again for a while.

Gaby felt his towel disappear from between them, felt his hard body against her.

Slowly he eased the pajama top above her hips and pressed a thigh between hers.

Heat washed her skin, and blood and

bones. "Jacques." With him, the loving was always fresh and uninhibited — and exquisite.

"I'm never going to let you go," he whispered against her neck. "You're mine, Gaby. All mine. Let me in, sweetheart."

Jacques held her hips and she felt the slipping of his skin on hers as he dipped behind her for an instant, then he filled her and the breath rushed from her lungs.

When the pajama top tugged at her elbows, Gaby struggled free and tossed it aside. She clutched the window rim and cried out her ecstasy. And her cries joined Jacques. With him, there would never be any sameness.

Their bodies rode together. If he hadn't held her, she would have fallen.

She heard her own voice, calling his name, before she gave herself up to the tide neither of them could stop.

"Do you remember what I told you . . . a long time ago?" Jacques said when the rippling aftershocks faded from their bodies. He carried her to the chaise and sat, cradling Gaby between his knees.

"You've told me a lot of things," she said. "But you can say them all again."

"It was about my grandfather. How he once told me I'd meet my nemesis.

"I remember."

"And I said I might explain what he meant one day."

She ran her fingers through the hair on his chest, traced it to his belly, and on.

Jacques trapped her finger. "Later, sweetheart. I'm only human. My grandfather was talking about my apparent reluctance to get married. I told him I wasn't interested because I hadn't met anyone I wanted to spend the rest of my life with."

Gaby looked at his handsome face in the faint moonlight. "You've got my attention."

"Grandfather said the choice would be taken out of my hands when I met this nemesis he was so sure existed for me somewhere."

"Go on."

"Gladly. I'm cold. How about you?"

"Sort of."

Jacques kissed her slowly, deeply, running his hands up and down her back and tangling them in her hair. "Maddening hatter," he murmured.

"What did you say?"

"I said, could I persuade the little nemesis I love to come to bed?"

Epilogue

"Well?"

"My god!" Jacques set his teeth.

"Does that mean you like it?"

He concentrated. "Maybe. Too soon to tell."

"But this has possibilities," she said.

"I'll have to run more complete tests before committing myself. Let me have some more." He glanced at her lowered eyelids, at flickering dark lashes and moist, parted lips.

"The cautious approach." She murmured, kneeling beside him. "I like that."

"Mmm, I wouldn't want to ruin my reputation."

"Really?"

"Really. But you're definitely getting to me." *Oh, yes, definitely.* "Mmm-mmm. That is . . . quite good. Maybe too much pleasure, too soon, isn't a great idea. Maybe I ought to be made to suffer — I mean, *savor* this very slowly."

She laughed. "Believe me, Jacques. I intend to take a very long time . . . not that I'm sure you'll hold out."

"You, madam, are presumptuous. I . . . ah." Sweet heaven, it was so damn good. "Lovely lady, you are one persuasive woman. I'm never going to get enough of this."

"Jacques, I'm going to unwrap some more goodies."

"Do it." The air was warm. He gradually filled his lungs. "This is certainly something new."

"Don't tell me there's anything Ledan hasn't done. You're trying to make me feel good."

"I do want to make you feel good. But this isn't just new . . . it's unique."

"There are always boundaries to be pushed." She hooked an elbow over his shoulder. "And we're going to keep right on pushing them. Tell me what you think of this."

He watched her peel away layers of delicate, lacy white.

"Interesting?" She lightly touched what she'd revealed.

"Beautiful," he said quietly. "Luscious. I'm starting to lose control here."

"Lose it. Let it go. But first I want my turn at tasting."

She bent over.

Jacques narrowed his eyes, crammed his jaws shut — and listened to the sounds of satisfaction. "Enough," he said at last. "Leave something for me to work with, huh?"

"You'll manage nicely." Raising her head, she pressed close. "Luscious, you said?"

"Yeah." He looked again at what she held, partly concealed with her fingers. "Good enough to eat."

"Great. Have you ever considered how much influence scent has on appeal?"

"Some."

"Tell me how the smell of this affects you?"

She knew what she was doing. Not a word had been spoken without careful consideration of the effect it would have on him. Jacques turned his face into softness.

"Oh, lady," he murmured. "I don't even know what the scent is, but I *like* it."

"Open your mouth."

Deliberately looking straight ahead, he did as she asked. She drew in a breath. "That's the way, Jacques. More. *More!*"

He tasted, tested textures with the tip of his tongue, and felt his senses slipping away.

She withdrew, evaded his grabbing hand. "Patience." She shifted. "Now this. Don't be greedy. Ah, oh, yes, *yes!* You like that as much as I do?"

Jacques sucked, willing his eyes to stay open.

"Tell me about it," she said.

He made a circle with his tongue and drew back to take a breath. "Smooth. But it's the hard center that really turns me on."

"Ever the man of great taste." She waited while he worked his lips and tongue some more. "And from what I'm looking at you're never going to have any difficulty rising to this kind of occasion."

Jacques shook his head, feeling vaguely drunk.

"You say you're the best judge," she told him. "Prove it. Tell me how to make this one unforgettable."

"You're not going to give me any time to think, are you?"

"No. You don't want me to. We have great ingredients here. I'd say the results are going to be better than our wildest dreams."

"You haven't seen my dreams. Ouch!"

"Sorry." She giggled. "Following an impulse."

"You'll kill both of us."

"No way. Trust me. Give me your hand."
He did as she asked.

"Feel this. Tell me what this is?"

"Silk?" Jacques's legs weakened. "And this is satin, pure satin. But I don't remember doing a test like this blind. Should I feel some more?"

"Oh, *yes.* Go ahead. It's all yours."

"The whole thing?"

"Uh-huh. Go on. Indulge yourself."

"This is a soft center," he said, barely able to breathe. "The best kind. Soft and sweet and just right."

Her cry closed his eyes. "You're definitely going to kill us both," he told her.

"What a hell of a way to go," she almost sobbed. "There's always something left to try, Jacques. And I've got an idea that's going to send you into orbit."

He believed her.

When she moved, it was so suddenly, he yelled and flailed. "You crazy female! What — ?"

White lace flew, yards and yards of white lace threaded with beige satin ribbon. Then Gaby sat astride his lap, the voluminous skirts of her wedding gown hiked up to her waist.

"Nut," he told her, grappling for control. Long, tight sleeves still clung demurely to her arms, but the tiny pearl buttons that had closed her bodice were no longer in use. Jacques looked directly at his wife's beautiful, naked breasts and clenched his muscles against arousal.

Gaby pulled off the white tie he'd already undone and opened his dress shirt. "I don't intend you ever to get bored." Her green, green eyes, glittered. "Are you bored?"

"No," he managed to sputter. "Afraid of imminent death, but not bored. Never bored with you. If you'll move, just a little, we might want to change one or two things about this treat."

"With pleasure."

He looked past her shoulder at a landscape that seemed to dip crazily. She was frying his mind — and other parts.

"Is this enough of a move?" Running her hands over her breasts, Gaby leaned back and looked down.

Heat exploded in him. The pale pink roses edging creamy silk stockings matched the flowers in her hair. Her garters were pink, too . . . almost the color of the puckered nipples on a level with his mouth.

"Okay, you crazy, sexy woman. *Finish it!*"

"With pleasure." She showed perfect, small teeth resting together. "Oh, Jacques, my love, always with pleasure."

Gaby had already made the necessary part of him available . . . and ready.

Jacques moved his right foot. "Wait!"

"I can't!"

Fragile pink panties tore. Gaby filled herself with him.

"Hell!"

The whole world exploded. Jacques's hips rose off the seat of their own accord. At the same instant he managed to slam on the brakes.

"Oh, hell," he heard himself shout. And he heard Gaby laugh while the Jeep shuddered to a stop.

In the seconds that followed, all he heard were Gaby's moans and his own rasping breath.

When the hot tide broke and rippled over them, he clasped her against him. "Most people would have waited till they got where they were going," he gasped into her wildly tossed hair.

"No fun."

"No," he agreed. "Not nearly as much fun. It's a good job I know this flat old road with my eyes closed."

"They were closed for a while there."

He gripped her arms and made enough space to allow him to see her. "Do you know how much I love you?"

"Yes. More than your life."

"Good. Do I know how much you love me?"

"Yes. More than my life."

"That's great. Glad we got it settled. Do you want to explain what made you decide to try and kill us in a Jeep on our wedding day?"

Gaby wiggled, with predictable results. "There was never any danger." She watched his eyes, his mouth, and leaned to kiss him slowly. "Mmm. So good. But Jeeps don't count."

"What?" Jacques struggled to sit straighter. "Jeeps don't count toward ultimate challenge," Gaby said, squinting thoughtfully. "But horseback will."

Stella Cameron is a national bestselling author of historical romances and mainstream women's fiction.

Readers love her character-driven stories of heartfelt emotion and everlasting romantic sentiment. Stella draws from people in her own life to create these memorable characters.

She now makes her home in Washington State.